The Yellow Dust

It all began on the way to Elkanville. Don Bancroft came across the body of Uncle Jeb and when he rode into town with the corpse he was greeted by the sheriff who was an old friend of his called Perce Maddison. But the murders didn't stop with Uncle Jeb and it wasn't long before Don was set up as the killer.

Nothing was quite as it seemed for friend became enemy and foe ended up as ally. Before the man responsible for five murders could be found and brought to justice, hot lead would fly and Don would have to face the lynch mob. Would peace ever return to Elkanville?

The Yellow Dust

Charlie Potts

A Black Horse Western

ROBERT HALE · LONDON

© Vic J. Hanson 1949, 2003
First hardcover edition 2003
Originally published in paperback as
The Yellow Dust by V. Joseph Hanson

ISBN 0 7090 7282 1

Robert Hale Limited
Clerkenwell House
Clerkenwell Green
London EC1R 0HT

Typeset by
Derek Doyle & Associates, Liverpool.
Printed and bound in Great Britain by
Antony Rowe Limited, Wiltshire

ONE

The buzzards circled and dipped and squabbled. Above them their ally, the sun, glared with noonday intensity. Below them, like pitiful bugs crawling on a hot plate – a hot plate laid with sand and rock and garnished with tortured vegetation – were a man, horse and a burro.

Two of the ungainly birds, bolder than their fellows, dipped lower, squealing at their intended prey as they flapped above their heads. The man raised his head and one arm, shaking his fist at them furiously. The pesky critters ought to know by now that Uncle Jeb wasn't their meat – he knew their domain too well – *he* would never be buzzard-bait.

The long hair that tumbled from beneath his battered slouch hat was snow white, but the red-rimmed eyes squinting against the sun-glare were bright with almost youthful fire and courage.

The blue haze before him was shifting now, and he could see the line of hills squatting like a row of puppies awaiting him. Beyond them was grass and water and, a few miles further on, his hometown. It wouldn't be long now. And this time he'd have some real news for the scoffers and headtappers and winkers, and those who, though always kind, he knew gently pitied him. The ol' desert-wolf was coming home with a bellyfull of richness, and tonight was his night to howl.

He wiped his face with a filthy bandanna, patting his cracked lips gingerly. He tried to spit away the sand that caked them, but that only hurt them more. He took a battered canteen from his saddle-horn, tipped it slightly and squinted into its depth. He grimaced. Then he took a short swig.

He replaced it. He patted his horse's neck and tried to say something but could only manage a hoarse croak. Pity there wasn't no water for ol' Kipper. Still, he'd lasted out as long as this many a time. And this would be his last trip. By cracky it would!

He squinted at the line of hills which seemed to hump and wriggle in the shimmering heat-haze. At times they looked like a mirage. But Uncle Jeb knew better.

He knew those hills too. He knew also that he still had quite a step to go. They were a damn sight further away than they seemed.

Nevertheless, to him, to this old desert-rat in his perfect time of triumph, they were but a jog-trot. He'd show the world! By cracky he would! He croaked jubilantly into the horse's ear and, as if he understood (and maybe he did after all their years together) the beast quickened his pace.

The old man's voice came back – it was not unusual for him to talk aloud to his horse. He said: 'There'll be green grass an' oats an' a quiet life for you, Kipper.'

The horse jerked his head as if to say, ' Thanks, ol' pard.'

Another hour passed before the old man tried to speak again and discovered he had lost his voice once more. He cast a speculative eye at the water canteen, then again at the hills before him. The heat was terrific. The hills danced. They seemed as far away as ever. The old man shrugged his bony shoulders, mechanically patted his mouth with his bandanna, patted Kipper's neck.

The sun's power became less. The hills came nearer. Still the old man did not drink. As long as he could hold out, he would. He still had a long way to go. He still had to get to the other side o' them pesky hills. The burro on the stout lead rope was lagging behind. The old man jerked the rope impatiently. With a subtle air of martyrdom the beast quickened his pace a little. He did not know that he, the last of a long line of Uncle Jeb's fabulous burros, carried the old man's life and dreams and salvation.

Overhead the buzzards still circled and cried petulantly, unheeded by the three old seasoned desert wanderers.

It was the burro, that lethargic, spavined four-legged freak, who first noticed the approaching rider. But when he turned his head slowly and slackened his pace, the old man only croaked a curse and pulled harder at the lead rope.

The buzzards' cries became shriller and more frenzied, and Kipper and his master turned to look.

The stranger was coming along at a steady jog-trot. The old man's hand dropped to the huge Colt at his hip. This tall rider with the wide-brimmed sombrero might be innocent – but Uncle Jeb wasn't taking any chances.

As the man came closer he waved a hand in greeting, and Jeb could see that he wore a dark bandanna over his mouth and nose to keep out the dust. It also effectively concealed his face. Nevertheless there was something familiar about him. And his horse too.

Then the newcomer called Jeb by name in a deep, muffled voice from beneath the bandanna.

The old man's hand came away from the butt of his gun, and he croaked a greeting. His eyes sparkled jubilantly. He indicated the burro's load of little sacks with proud and extravagant gestures. That this man, a friend and yet a scoffer, should be the first to hear of his good fortune, was good to his soul.

The rider came on more slowly, nodding his head understandingly. The old man thought that he was smiling beneath his protective mask.

It was when he sensed the rider was no longer smiling, and he saw his hand was moving swiftly, that the old man realized his mistake.

His brain was trigger-quick, but his limbs were old and did not obey so swiftly. His draw was slow, and his gun was barely out of its sheath when the other man fired.

The slug hit the old man in the chest. For a moment he swayed, his eyes wide with agony, and loathing, and a dreadful accusation. Then he coughed and fell from the saddle.

Terrified, the horse, Kipper, started forward. The man fired again. The horse stopped dead. Its front knees gave way and then, with a sigh almost human, it fell on its side.

The burro stood stolidly, its lead-rope slack. The buzzards' din was hideous. They smelt blood.

The killer worked swiftly. He stripped the burro of its burden, emptying the little sacks and transferring the dull, uninteresting looking metal, which gleamed a little here and there, to his own capacious saddle-bags.

He remounted his horse. Relieved of his load, the burro stood in a sagging attitude. The man drew his gun once more and shot it in the side of the head. Then he wheeled his mount and, without a backward glance, galloped away.

He did not see the old man raise himself on to his elbows and begin to crawl. With superhuman courage and endurance he crawled quite a way from the bodies of the burro and horse before he finally stopped and fell forward on his face once more. And there, in the desolate places where he had lived and worked and dreamed, he died.

The light began to wane, and the first buzzard plopped clumsily down a few yards from the body and began to waddle cautiously nearer.

He was only a few feet away when his companions, who were descending on the carcasses of the horse and burro, began to utter warning cries and rise again. The lone buzzard paused uncertainly, he was loth to give up his prize. His companions' cries became shriller and as their panic communicated itself to him, he rose ungainly.

A shot echoed, and he seemed to pause once more in midair, one wing drooping grotesquely. Then he fell like a stone, to land with a full final thud a few yards from his erstwhile prey.

Don Bancroft smiled mirthlessly and lowered his rifle. He had a feeling of savage satisfaction, the certainty of an evil thing destroyed.

He passed the bodies of the horse and burro with a glance, his look becoming stern again as he approached the third and most pitiful bundle.

He dismounted and went on his knees beside the body. His hard, weather-beaten face with its three-days growth of

9

stubble, crinkled a little with a sudden sadness as he noticed the already drying stain on the old man's breast.

Elkanville was an up-and-coming little cowtown. It was situated in the centre of a wide belt of lush grassland and was at the head of a branch line running from the junction at Austin. Its people and their friends from the neighbouring ranches were prosperous and complacent. Their only grouse was that Elkanville was too near the border and the desert and, consequently, a haven for outlaws. These hung around town, sometimes for months, vanishing into the desert and so across the border at the first signs of pursuit. Hard-looking saddle-tramps came and went incessantly. They were the sort of people who resented questions in no uncertain manner. So the good people of Elkanville watched them come and go, shrugged their shoulders the while – what the heck, so long as they were passably well behaved they were welcome. They brought trade to the town (of a kind), the honky-tonks kept a-booming. An' if they didn't behave – well, what was the sheriff paid for? He was the fastest-drawin' man hereabouts. He oughta keep his hand in.

A stranger at night was no rare occurrence, but as this disreputable-looking ranny on the raw-boned nag passed the lighted windows, and it became evident what manner of burden he carried, interest was quickened. A small crowd had collected when he dismounted outside the sheriff's office and gently eased his burden down.

The onlookers pressed forward.

'Gosh, it's Uncle Jeb Carter,' said somebody.

The word passed around. Uncle Jeb Carter dead – murdered most likely – brought in by a hard-looking stranger. Ignoring the crowd, disdaining to answer shouted questions, Bancroft carried the body across the boardwalk to the office. The watchers noted that he walked lopsidedly as if one leg were shorter than the other. As he kicked the door it opened, and he was confronted by a lean individual with a halo of red hair framed by the lamplight behind him. Without a word this man stepped aside to allow Bancroft to enter. Then he closed the door behind him. He, too, ignored the crowd.

Bancroft carried the body across the office past the huge, battered desk and placed it gently on the couch against the wall.

He turned. 'You the sheriff?'

'No, I'm Pete Otson, the deputy. The sheriff ain't here.' The red-headed beanpole took a few paces forward and stood over the body.

'Found him out on the desert,' said Bancroft. 'Late this afternoon. Figured he hadn't bin dead long. Buzzards were only jest droppin'. They hadn't touched him. His horse an' burro'd both bin shot. Lot of little bags strewed about. Whoever did it took the ol' man's haul.'

'You don't mean to tell me thet ol' Uncle Jeb had struck it rich after all these years?'

'Suttinly looked like it. There wuz a sprinklin' o' gold dust in them bags. Didn't know the ol' man wuz your uncle.'

'He ain't. Everybody calls him uncle around these parts. He's got no kin as I know of. He's bin prospectin' ever since I was a nipper, an' he always came back empty handed. Any clues or ideas, stranger?'

'Only what I told yuh.'

Pete Otson bent over the body and began to feel in the pockets of the worn vest.

'I guess I'll go an' get some supper,' said Bancroft. 'Can you recommend a place?'

The deputy looked up. 'You could try Tiger Macintosh's, five doors away.'

'All right. Thanks. I'll be there if you want me.'

Otson grunted. Bancroft left the office. He wended his way through the loungers who still stood about outside.

He spotted the name 'Tiger Macintosh' on a weather-beaten hanging sign and entered through the battered door beneath it, into a long, low place smelling not unpleasantly of well-cooked food.

Tiger himself, a huge, middle-aged man with a battered face and a bald head, took his order.

Bancroft did justice to the meal that was placed before him by a little Chinaman and was leaning back and rolling a quirly when he heard somebody say: 'Here's the sheriff.'

He looked up at the big, well-built blond-haired man who came through the door.

Their eyes met. Recognition dawned. The sheriff's handsome face split in a grin.

'By all that's holy. Gimpy Bancroft!' he said. He strode forward, hand outstretched.

TWO

Bancroft stood up. His lips quirked, light dawned in his sombre eyes. He grasped the large, well-kept hand and shook it heartily.

'Perce Maddison!' he ejaculated. 'I never expected to meet you here. An' sheriff, too—'

'Yuh durn tootin',' grinned Maddison. 'An' yuh don't mean to tell me you're the *hombre* I came here to find – you found old Uncle Jeb?'

'Yuh durn tootin',' echoed Bancroft, but his voice was sober.

He sat down again. The sheriff pulled up a chair. Briefly, Bancroft told him of how he had found Jeb Carter. He reiterated the fact that the murderer had left no trace apart from, probably, the bullet.

Maddison blew out his breath in distress.

'Poor old Jeb,' he said. 'I'd like to get my hands on the polecat who did it. If you say there's no clues, Gimpy, there ain't. An old Injin fighter like you oughta be able to read sign by now. I'll hafta ride out there an' have a look – jest public sayso, y'understand? But I guess the only chance I've got is if somebody starts passin' gold around the district.' He paused. 'What d'yuh say to a drink? Can't get

13

any good hooch in this place. C'mon over to the Buckeye Bar.'

The two men rose. Bancroft followed the sheriff across the dusty, rutted-mud street, through pools of light and shade and through the batwings of a garish saloon. People greeted the sheriff. Curious glances followed the two men as they crossed the floor to the bar. Both were tall and of about the same age – in their thirties. Sheriff Maddison was the heavier built of the two; Bancroft was lean and hard. They were a formidable-looking pair.

They breasted the bar, side by side like the old pards they were, Maddison's left foot touching Bancroft's on the brass rail as the former ordered drinks from a grinning bartender.

They were drinking and talking over old times when a dark, tubby man came along the bar and spoke to Maddison.

The sheriff introduced him to Bancroft as Mike Calhoun, owner of the Buckeye Bar. Calhoun had a round, rosy face and a deep, attractive voice.

He greeted Bancroft pleasantly and then, turning once more to the sheriff, said, 'What's this I hear about ol' Jeb Carter being kilt?'

'It's a fact,' said Maddison soberly. 'He's in the office. Gimpy, here, brought him in. Found him out on the desert.'

Calhoun gave Bancroft another sharp look from his little eyes in their puckered pouches. Then he said to Maddison: 'Wal, what are yuh gonna do about it?' His tone was still pleasantly conversational, but he obviously expected some kind of an answer.

The sheriff grinned. But his eyes remained cold. He

said: 'Wal, Gimpy's gonna take me out there to show me where he found the body. Although he says there are no clues.'

'So,' said Calhoun.

He spoke now as if Bancroft were not there. The lean ranny kept his mouth shut, but his hard eyes watched the two men.

Calhoun called across the bar to the barman to 'set 'em up.'

Only when they had their drinks in their hands and Bancroft wished the tubby man 'good health' did Calhoun turn to him once more.

He said: 'How come you found ol' Jeb?'

Bancroft figured it was a kind of silly question to ask and Calhoun had no right to question him anyway. He felt like retorting sharply, but held his tongue in check.

'The buzzards led me to the spot. They'd got to work on the horse an' burro, but they hadn't touched the ol' man.'

Calhoun seemed satisfied and began to talk commonplaces. A queer cuss. He suddenly excused himself and left the two men.

Shortly afterwards Bancroft and Sheriff Maddison left the Buckeye Bar.

They were stepping off the boardwalk on to the hard-baked mud when a one-horse gig came careering down the street, and the horse reared to a halt directly in front of them, causing them both to step back in alarm. The light streaming from the windows of the saloon bathed the scene. A girl looked down at them from the seat of the gig and said: 'Is it true, Perce, that Uncle Jeb has been murdered?'

'I'm afraid so, Miriam,' replied Maddison.

The girl lifted a firm chin. 'I must tell father,' she said.

She jerked the reins. The gig careered off again. Its wheels sent a cloud of dust into the faces of the two men.

'Phew,' said Bancroft. He had had a confused glimpse of a trim figure, reddish-gold curls glinting in the light, and a pretty – almost boyish – face. That was all.

'That's Miriam Burgoyne,' Maddison told him. 'Her father, ol' Burt, is the Grand Panjandrum around here. He owns almost everythin' – an' rules it. But he's a good man – a real ol' fire-breathin' Puritan. It was him who nominated me fer sheriff.' He grinned wryly: 'I couldn't lose.'

They walked along the street to his office. Little knots of people still hung around in the dusk. They eyed the two men curiously. Nobody spoke.

Maddison said: 'Everybody liked ol' Jeb. He was a crazy ol' coot. But harmless.'

'He wuz that crazy he found a bonanza,' said Bancroft.

They entered the office. With the deputy sheriff, Pete Otson, was another man and a youth. The latter, tow-headed and gangling, was sitting on the edge of the desk, his freckled cheeks bulged out by a mysterious something he was masticating slowly. All they could see of the man was a pair of legs like tree-trunks and a huge billowing back as he bent over the body of the old prospector.

'Get off that desk, Pinky,' said Maddison.

The youth grinned and slid to a leaning position, his long legs spread out in front of him.

The huge fat man turned, revealing a perfectly round, flabby face, red with the exertion of bending.

'Hi-yuh, Sheriff.'

Maddison introduced the fat man to Bancroft as

16

'Three-ton Thurston, the biggest burial expert in the United States.' Bancroft's hand disappeared in the other's huge red pad and he winced at the undertaker's grip.

'All right, Pinky,' said Three-ton Thurston.

The youth dragged forth something Bancroft had not noticed before, a plain deal coffin. Pinky removed the lid, and the man and the boy gently lowered the remains of the old man into the box.

Thurston's face was puce-like when he straightened up.

'Slug from a forty five did the job,' he said briefly, panting a little.

Pinky fitted the lid on. Thurston bent once more. Deputy Otson opened the door for them and they carried the coffin out

It was the following morning. Gentle, early morning. Once more the scene was set in the sheriff's office in Elkanville. There sat Bancroft, Maddison and Otson.

Sheriff Perce Maddison said: 'Me an' Gimpy are gonna ride out to where he found ol' Jeb.'

Deputy Sheriff Pete Otson said: 'All right. I'll look after things here.'

Horses' hoofs clattered outside, stopped. Footsteps sounded, then a knock on the door.

'Come in.'

A little wizened cowhand entered.

'The boss wants tuh see yuh, Sheriff,' he said 'Urgent.'

Maddison opened his mouth to say something, closed it, paused, opened it again, and said:

'All right, Shorty. I'll come now. You goin' right back?'

'Nope. I got the day off. I'm gonna stay in town. Adios.'

As the door closed behind him, the sheriff turned to

Bancroft. 'I'm sorry, Gimpy, I gotta go. Take Pete with yuh.'

'All right,' Bancroft said. There seemed to be a helluva lot of coming and going.

Maddison left. Bancroft said to the deputy: 'Who was the little *hombre*?'

'Shorty Matthews, one of Burt Burgoyne's rannies.'

Bancroft grunted. Then he said: 'Wal, are you ready tuh go ridin', Pete?'

'Jest as soon as you say.'

The two men left the office. Deputy Otson locked up. Then they went and got their horses from the stables out back and rode out of town.

As they took the trail Bancroft said: 'I suppose this Burgoyne cuss has got a big place, ain't he?'

'The Curly W,' said Otson. 'Biggest ranch in the district. Ol' man Burgoyne owns lots of other places besides the Curly W—'

'Yeh, so Perce Maddison said – I suppose that's where Perce's gone, ain't it?'

'Sure thing. When ol' Burt says urgent, Perce goes a-runnin'. He's a good guy is Perce, but he has to kow-tow to the Burgoynes a bit. Ol' man's very powerful – an' I guess Perce's kinda sweet on his daughter.'

'That'd be Miriam.'

'Yeh. You met her?'

'Wal, not exactly.' Bancroft told the deputy of his whirl-wind introduction to the reckless and imperious Miss Burgoyne.

'She's a tartar,' decided Otson. 'Nothin' agin her, mind yuh. She's jest wild an' likes all her own way. The apple of ol' Burt's eye. Only child now, yuh see. He had a son who got kilt in a gamblin' ruckus in Austin 'bout four years ago. The ol' man's only been tuh town a few times since then. Shuts himself away at the ranch. Ain't got no time for the townsfolk – hates most of 'em like pizen – 'cept the sheriff an' ol' Uncle Jeb. For some reason, he was very fond of ol' Jeb. I guess that's why he wants to see Perce in such a sure-fire hurry.'

The grassland over which they rode now was getting poorer, sparse and interspersed by dry patches of sand or rock. About half a mile in front of them lay the humpy line of the hills; beyond them was the desert. The sun was approaching its zenith. Above the hills was a bluish dusty heat-haze.

'Yuh say ol' Burgoyne has plenty of property in town,' said Bancroft. 'Who looks after it for him, if he don't come there himself?'

'Kit Hamden, his foreman,' said Otson soberly. 'The man who wields the whip in the ol' man's place.'

'Sounds ominous,' said Bancroft. 'What kind of a *hombre* is this Kit Hamden?'

'Got nothin' agin him,' said Otson. 'Jest don't like the cuss. He's a leech – an' a smooth-talkin', panty-waisted galoot.'

The other man's lips quirked. 'Nothin' agin him,' he echoed softly.

The deputy shrugged. 'Perce hates his guts. Mostly 'cos he's so pally with Miriam Burgoyne, I guess. Nothin' settled, y'understand? But it's certainly working that way. Hamden's sittin' pretty. As long as he'll squeeze the tenants till they squeal, the ol' man'll love him like a son.'

'An' does the daughter favour him?'

'Cain't say – cain't say. Guess the gal likes to dangle 'em

a little.' The deputy grinned. 'She's mighty purty. She could dangle me any time.'

Bancroft grinned with him. He was getting to like this garrulous, free-and-easy, red-topped beanpole.

The two men passed through a narrow gap in the hills, the clip-clop of their horses' hoofs echoing beyond. Out into the open again, and the desert was before them. They rode in single file along a narrow trail bordered by prickly cacti. Otson took the lead.

One moment there was the silence of the open spaces; the next, something buzzed by Bancroft's ear; then came the flat echoes of a rifle-shot and deputy Pete Otson pitched from his horse. Bancroft turned in his saddle; his hand dipped, his gun appeared. Silence once more, and no sign of life.

He turned his horse and rode boldly forward a little way, looking up at the hills before him. Suddenly, from the narrow defile through which he and the deputy had just passed, came a clatter of hoofs. Bancroft kneed his horse to a gallop, rode recklessly through the gap. At the other end he could see the green of the grass and the blue sky meeting it; and, outlined on this natural backcloth, the dark pigmy figures of a man and horse.

Bancroft cursed softly between his teeth. The man had too big a start to be caught. And Otson might be badly hurt. He wheeled his horse and returned at a gallop.

The deputy lay in a recumbent heap, his horse grazing nearby as if nothing had happened. Bancroft dismounted and went clown on his knees beside the still, crumpled man. He ripped the bloodstained shirt at the breast swiftly aside. His hand was warm and sticky as he felt for the pulse. It was still beating slightly. But there was a dangerous wound in the shoulder, not so far from the heart. And the deputy was losing a lot of blood.

Almost frenziedly, Bancroft tore away at his own shirt, ripped it off and into strips.

He wadded the wound to staunch the blood, and bound the shoulder, chest and back tightly, grunting as he tightened the knots. It was rough work, but he hoped it would prove effective until he got Otson back to town.

He lifted the man gently. He was better off as he was – unconscious. He lifted him on to his own horse, laying him as flat and as comfortably as possible, and tying him on with the long reata from his own saddle-horn.

THREE

Doc Penders, Elkanville's one and only medico, grunted as he straightened his broad back. In his hand he held a bloodstained lump of metal.

'Sharp's rifle slug,' he said laconically. His voice was deep.

His dark, handsome, dissipated features wore a sardonic look. The women of the town said he had no heart and soul, and that he had a bad past. They could not prove it, however. The men trusted and were a little in awe of him. He was a good man at his job – in a different class to the failures and drunkards often found getting a precarious living as general practitioners in such towns as Elkanville.

He carried a gun in a shoulder-holster. And he could shoot.

He was finishing the job on Otson when the deputy came to.

'What hit me?' he said. Then he saw Bancroft. 'Gimpy—'

'We wuz bushwhacked the other side o' the hills.'

'Who—?'

Bancroft shook his head. 'He hightailed. Got too much

of a start. I had tuh see to you.'

'Thanks, Gimpy—'

Doc Penders said: 'You'll be all right. Rest's the thing now. Bed. I've sent for a buggy.'

'Thanks, Doc.' Otson turned his head to look again at Bancroft. 'I've got a room at Calamity Kate's in the main drag. Better go there.'

'All right.'

The doctor left the room. When he came back he said: 'The buggy's here.'

'I can walk,' said Otson. 'I can manage. Thanks again, Doc.'

'Forget it.'

Bancroft saw Otson to the buggy, driven by a grizzled, baccy-chewing old-timer. The doctor was standing at the doorway of his frame bungalow. Bancroft returned to him.

'What do I owe yuh, Doc?'

'Forget it. Otson's a good *hombre*.'

Two pairs of hard eyes met in a single glance. Then their owners turned in their separate directions. 'Send for me if you want me,' Penders called over his shoulder.

Calamity Kate's rooming-house was a three story place, part brick, part wood frame. When Bancroft brought the wounded man in, she did not ask questions but led the way upstairs. She was middle-aged and mannish, tough and efficient.

When Otson was comfortably tucked between the sheets, Bancroft introduced himself to the tall, ugly woman.

She gripped his hand. 'Pete told me about you,' she said. 'Glad to meet yuh.'

Then Bancroft told her of how they were dry-gulched.

'Any idea who done it?'

'Nope, not a clue.'

Bancroft left Calamity's and went to his room at Tiger Macintosh's. He had a meal sent up to him, and put in a spell of thinking while he ate. After a good meal he felt better, but his puzzling had got him exactly no place.

He reckoned he'd better go and see if Perce Maddison had returned from Burgoyne's Curly W and, if he had, report the affair to him.

As he left Tiger's, the sheriff came riding down the street. He reined in.

'I met Doc Penders on the trail. He tells me Otson's bin shot.'

'Yeh,' said Bancroft. He wondered where Penders was making for.

'Come into the office, Gimpy.'

Bancroft caught hold of the horse's bridle. Maddison dismounted and they walked together.

Hoofs cluttered behind them. The horse crashed to a stop, enveloping them in dust. The sheriff and his friend turned savagely.

From the saddle of a huge ginger mare a young, arrogant, dark-faced waddy looked down at them.

'Oh, it's you, Kit,' said Maddison without warmth. 'In a kind of hurry, ain't yuh?'

'Not now,' said the younker. 'What's this I hear about Deputy Otson bein' plugged?'

'If you'll come to the office we'll hear more about it,' said Maddison.

'All right.'

The young man did not dismount, but paced his horse

24

with them. The beast was restive and continued to kick up dust.

Bancroft said: 'Maybe you'd better light down, mister. A bellyful o' dirt won't go well with the meal I've just eaten.'

'I don't like walkin',' said the other softly.

The sheriff said: 'Don't start anything, Hamden.'

For answer the rider dug spurs into his horse. The beast reared, and as the dust rose thicker broke into a gallop.

Bancroft cursed and spat, reaching for his gun. Maddison grasped his wrist.

Bancroft shrugged. 'All right, Perce,' he said. 'But that's all you'll stop me doin'.'

They reached the office to find the ginger mare tied to the hitching-post outside. The dark young man lounged against the door.

He didn't smile as he said: 'Took yuh kind of a long time, gents.'

The sheriff ignored him and turned to tie up his own horse. Bancroft strode towards the young man. The younker came away from the door. Bancroft hit him flush in the mouth with his open palm.

The younker staggered, his heavy body hitting the door with a thud. He righted himself, his mouth contorted, his eyes blazing. His hand sped downwards.

His gun was out of its sheath when Bancroft fired from the hip. The younker cried out in agony, clutching his gun-hand. The weapon clattered on the sidewalk a few yards away.

Bancroft stepped out of the young man's path.

'Get on your hoss,' he said. His eyes glowed strangely. He jerked the gun. 'Quick. Before I blow one o' your ears off.'

25

Watching him with hate-filled eyes, the young man passed and remounted his horse. Then he spoke, addressing Maddison.

'You saw that, Sheriff. He struck the first blow.'

'You asked for it,' said Maddison.

'You'll both hear more about this,' the young man snarled. He set his horse at a gallop and went down the street in a cloud of dust.

Maddison said: 'Wal, Gimpy, you jest met Kit Hamden, Bart Burgoyne's right-hand man.'

'Yeh, so I gathered,' said Bancroft. 'Although he looked younger than I expected.'

'He wears well. An' you mustn't under-estimate him, Gimpy. He's purty deadly. An' powerful – I hate to think what ol' Burt'll have tuh say about this.'

'Don't let it worry yuh, Sheriff,' said Bancroft with a half-smile.

He picked up Hamden's gun. The barrel was twisted where the slug had struck it. With a careless gesture he tossed it away from him.

'Hamden's got plenty more guns – an' fingers to pull 'em,' said Maddison cryptically. 'Next time you might not have a chance to beat him tuh the draw. He probably won't be there tuh beat.'

'You needn't talk in riddles, Perce,' Bancroft told him. 'I get your drift. An' does your puritanical Mr Burt Burgoyne condone dry-gulchin'?'

'He gives Hamden purty well a free hand, I guess,' said the sheriff. 'An' what he don't hear about he cain't grieve about—'

'An' that's the ol' buzzard you're backin'?'

'Nope! He's backin' me.'

'You're an irritatin' cus, Perce,' said Bancroft, but there was no rancour in his voice.

The two men sat opposite each other at the big desk, and Bancroft told the sheriff of how Pete Otson had got shot.

'No clue this time either,' said Maddison.

'No.'

'An' did yuh reach the place where Uncle Jeb wuz shot?'

'No, we didn't get that far. I figure it wuz the same guy who shot Uncle Jeb who bushwhacked us too. Maybe there was somethin' out there he didn't want us to see. Maybe there was a clue there after all, an' I missed it.'

'That what you figure?'

'Wal, what else is there? Why else should anybody shoot at me an' Pete?'

'Yeh, that suttinly takes some figurin',' said Maddison. He produced two quirlies and handed one to Bancroft. They lit up.

Boot-heels slammed on the boardwalk outside. The door was rapped, then immediately opened.

Tubby Mike Calhoun, owner of the Buckeye Bar, strode in. 'What's this I hear, Sheriff,' he said, 'about Pete Otson gettin' shot?'

'Lots o' people seem tuh be askin' that question,' said Bancroft sardonically.

The saloon owner glared at him.

'No call tuh come bargin' in here like a ten-cent stick-up man, Mike,' said the sheriff. 'Sit down. We wuz jest talkin' about Pete.' He turned to Bancroft. 'Mike's kind of unofficial mayor around here, Gimpy. Very public spirited. He likes to know what's goin' on.'

Bancroft grinned. 'Mr Calhoun always comes along jest after I've told my story.'

Just for the sake of keeping peace he figured he'd best tell the tale again to the tubby man. Briefly he did so.

When he had finished, Mr Calhoun merely grunted. He sat silent for a moment then, pointedly ignoring Bancroft, he turned to the sheriff and said softly:

'Seems to me this man's always around when somebody gets shot. I jest heard that he blasted Kit Hamden.'

'Hamden asked for it,' said the sheriff. 'I can vouch for Gimpy. He's an old friend o' mine.'

'How old?'

'We wuz kids together.'

'An' you hadn't seen him since then till he blew in town yesterday with Jeb Carter's body.'

'Wal, no, but—'

'I thought so.' Calhoun's well-modulated voice was full of triumph. 'I guess—'

The rest of his sentence was a mere gurgle as a large hand gripped his black cravat, twisting it tight. He was lifted to his feet and swivelled round, his eyes bulging until he looked into the hard face and cold eyes of Gimpy Bancroft.

'You've got a nasty habit of talking about people as if they ain't there, mister,' said Bancroft. 'An' sayin' nasty things about people, too. I don't like it.'

'Gimpy,' said the sheriff warningly.

Bancroft ignored him.

He shoved Calhoun, letting go suddenly of the cravat. The plump saloon owner was catapulted across the room to land with a crash on the floor against the wall.

He wriggled himself slowly into a sitting position. Then

his hand darted beneath the lapel of his double-breasted jacket. Bancroft's hand dipped more swiftly. His Colt boomed deafeningly in the little office. The slug took a chunk of cloth from the shoulder of Calhoun's coat.

The saloon owner froze, his hand now clutching his lapel. His eyes bulged, his ruddy face began to change colour as he watched the gun that was trained at his head.

Once more Bancroft's eyes glowed with that strange light.

He said: 'Dip down for that gun, Mr Calhoun, an' bring it forth gently between thumb and forefinger. Then jest toss it towards me.'

Calhoun's hand was far from steady as he brought forth, in the manner prescribed, a snub-nosed derringer. He tossed it at Bancroft's feet. The tall man bent, picked it up and tucked it in his belt.

'Get up,' he said. 'And get out.'

Calhoun rose to his feet. His eyes darted from Bancroft to the sheriff and back again. He opened his mouth to say something, changed his mind, turned on his heel and left the office. The door banged behind him.

Bancroft looked at the sheriff.

'You shouldn't have done that, Gimpy,' the sheriff said.

'Why? Is he another pard of yours?'

'No. I've never liked him. But he is somebody in this town. What he wuz sayin' about you was jest hot air. It didn't mean a thing. I'm used to it.'

'Seems to me there's a lot of things you're kinda used to, Perce,' said Bancroft levelly.

'I've learnt to use a lot of tact and diplomacy,' the sheriff said. 'Sometimes it pays better than force.'

'When a man insults me I know only one thing to do,'

said Bancroft curtly. 'You'd better warn some o' the big shots in this town o' yourn, Perce. If anybody else starts tuh ride me I'm liable to kill 'em.'

He turned on his heel in the wake of Calhoun.

'Gimpy,' said Maddison.

But again the door banged.

FOUR

Bancroft wanted a drink. He figured it would be unwise to visit the Buckeye Bar right now. Its owner would be kinda reluctant to serve a guy who'd just batted his ears down.

Bancroft went to Tiger Macintosh's. Tiger's eats were first rate, but his liquor was pure poison. Still, right now Bancroft felt so ornery, as well as thirsty, that he figured he could drink anything. Also, drinking hours were pretty irregular at Tiger's; you could get it almost any time!

The bald-headed ex-pug greeted him with a wide grin.

'Soon back,' he said.

'Yeh, ain't much to do in this town,' said Bancroft with a thin smile. 'Set 'em up an' have one with me.'

He took his liquor and downed it with Tiger's best wishes. He took the bottle and poured himself another glass. He indicated Tiger's glass with a jerk of the bottle.

'No more for me, thanks,' said the ex-pug. 'I don't drink much in working hours.'

Bancroft smiled and shrugged. He turned, while Tiger polished glasses and surveyed the room. It was fairly full of late diners and a few drinkers. As he watched, the door opened and four men strode in. They stood on the threshold and looked around the room, then strode to the bar

31

beside Bancroft. They were tough-looking customers.

They greeted Tiger and called for drinks. Tiger greeted them by their names, though not over-enthusiastically, it seemed, as he served them. He turned back to his glass-polishing.

The man who stood nearest to Bancroft was big and unshaven, with the beginnings of a swelling under-carriage. He turned and looked at the lone man and leered.

'Howdy, pardner,' he said.

Bancroft had seen him before knocking around town, mostly in the Buckeye Bar.

'Howdy,' he said.

'That's the stranger who finds all the bodies, ain't it, Lou?' said one of the other men.

'Yeh,' said Lou. 'They tell me he's a reg'lar ringtailed bob-cat.' His manner was patently insulting.

This is it, thought Bancroft. Calhoun ain't wasted any time. Well, if it had gotta come it might as well be outside. He put down his empty glass.

'I'm sorry I can't stay an' converse with yuh,' he said. 'I gotta be moseying along.'

Lou moved his bulk in front of him.

'What's the matter?' he said. 'Don't yuh wanta answer some questions? Strangers in this town allus haf to answer questions. Specially when they keep bein' around when somebody gets shot. It looks kinda suspicious—'

'Does it, brother?' said Bancroft. 'Wal, I guess that's jest my bad luck. I gotta get moving now. Would yuh mind jest stepping a little bit to one side?'

Lou grinned and stayed put. Out of the corner of his eye Bancroft saw the other three edging nearer. So they don't want it on the street, he thought. Too public maybe. Well, this was it . . . .

Then a voice said: 'I want no trouble in here, gents.'

Bancroft saw Lou's eyes bulge out of his head. He turned. Tiger Macintosh was grinning across the bar. In each of his gnarled fists was a huge Frontier-model Colt.

Then Bancroft saw something else. He opened his mouth to shout as the farthest of the four men slung a bottle. It struck Tiger on the side of his head. The Colts clattered on top of the bar and the big ex-pug sagged. Blood stained his bald scalp.

Bancroft went for his guns. But he never reached them. Lou's fist hit him flush in the mouth.

As he staggered back against the bar, his head spinning, his face a ball of sickening agony, the thought flashed through his mind. They haven't had orders to kill me then, just to rough me around a bit.

As Lou advanced on him he lifted his foot and kicked him in his protruding under-carriage. The big man gave a horrible grunting cry and doubled up. Bancroft brought his knee up into the lowering face as the man went down.

He ducked a blow aimed at the side of his head by the second man. He swung a haymaker and had the satisfaction of feeling his knuckles bite into the man's cheek and seeing him go down. Then the other man was advancing and behind him, the last one of the quartet was facing the room with two guns drawn, daring anyone else to interfere.

Bancroft met the third man. He was a heavily built youngster. They swapped punches, and Bancroft realized he was up against somebody now who needed watching. A fist crashed through his guard bringing searing agony once more to his mutilated lips.

As he righted himself the second man rose from the floor and tackled him round the waist. Bancroft hit him viciously on the back of the neck, at the same time warding off with his elbow another blow the younker slung at him.

Both men broke away, exchanged glances and came in again. The younker dodged a blow and retaliated with one which, although it missed its intended mark, numbed the muscle of Bancroft's left arm. Then the younker's pard kicked Bancroft on the knee-cap. The rangy man hissed with agony, his leg gave way entirely, and he went down on one knee. Two blows from the younker hit him in the face, and he went over on his back.

They waited for him to get up. Even as he climbed to his feet he knew his one leg wouldn't hold him. The pain from the battered kneecap was excruciating, and the leg itself felt like putty. He launched himself at the two, butting the dangerous young man in the stomach. The younker grunted and sank to his knees, clutching his midriff.

A hand gripped Bancroft's shoulder from behind, jerking him to his feet and swinging him around. Lou had wakened up.

Bancroft was slung against the bar and Lou hit him. Once, twice. Slapping his head from side to side like a rag doll. The other two men came forward and blows rained on the lone man. He no longer felt them. When he sagged Lou's hand held hits up.

Then a voice cut through it all, impinging on Bancroft's blurred consciousness like a knife-stab.

'*Stop it!*'

The blows no longer fell. Through half-closed eyes Bancroft saw the man with the guns by the bar drop them. He saw the other two-gun man by the door coming nearer. It was Perce Maddison.

The sheriff said: 'All right, Gimpy. Look after this man somebody.'

Men, now no longer menaced, rose from the tables to help the beaten man.

'You four, walk in front o' me,' said the sheriff. 'Take it easy now.'

'Thanks, Perce,' croaked Bancroft.

He had a confused impression of being carried upstairs by two men and being placed on the bed in his own room. Then he remembered no more.

He came to his senses coughing and spluttering, raw whiskey searing his bursted lips and stopping the breath in his throat. Tiger Macintosh, with a bottle in his hand, was grinning down at him.

'How're yuh feeling?' he said.

'Fine,' said Bancroft, wincing at every movement of his lips and facial muscles. 'How are you?'

'Jest a scratch,' grinned Tiger. 'C'mon, sit up if you can so's I can patch you up.'

Bancroft eased himself laboriously into a sitting position. Pain from his knee shot up into his groin like a jet of scalding water. He was getting the room into focus now and could see that on the little bedside table were bandages, ointment and a steaming bowl of water.

'Doc Penders is outa town. So you'll have tuh put up with me for the first treatment,' said Tiger.

'All right, old-timer. Begin the torture.'

And torture it was. Both men cursing; Tiger because he wasn't used to being a nurse and was very clumsy withal; Bancroft because it was simpler than yelling aloud at the ex-pug's ministrations.

Tiger enlivened the proceedings, however, by describing how he came round just in time to see the four bruisers being marched down the street at gun-point by the sheriff, who clapped them in the hoosegow. They were to be tried the following morning by Judge Gorter for assault and battery and disturbing the peace.

'Who's Judge Gorter?' asked Bancroft.

Tiger shrugged. 'Smelly ol' cuss. Big pard o' Calhoun's.'

'So that's that.'

'It looks like it,' said Tiger. 'But don't you fret none, pardner. Me an' you'll get even somehow.'

He was still grinning hideously, showing the gaps in his broken teeth. He'd probably grin at the mouth of hell. He was a fighter, and Bancroft admired him.

The admiration was mutual.

The ex-pug bound the damaged knee while the man on the bed called him all the unprintable names he could think of. Spanish and Indian ones as well as English. Tiger's grin widened so that it threatened to split his craggy visage in two.

He looked at a long jagged scar on Bancroft's sinewy thigh.

'Got that climbing when I wuz a kid,' said the lean ranny. 'I've limped ever since.'

'That's why Maddison calls yuh Gimpy, I guess.'

'Yeh, he was there when I done it. The nick-name's stuck ever since.'

'Names will,' said the ex-pug. 'When I first went into the ring I was a hot-blooded rip 'em an' tear 'em young cuss. That's why they labelled me Tiger.' He shook his bald head ruefully. 'Maybe I'd've gone further if I'd had more science. I guess I don't stop and think so much now if it comes to that, or I wouldn't 've got mahself crowned with a bottle this afternoon. I'm shore sorry I—'

'Forget it,' Bancroft told him. 'I guess if you hadn't bin laid out so early we'd 've wiped the boards with them four *hombres.*'

'Shore would,' grinned Tiger. 'By all accounts you put up one helluva battle.'

'P'raps we'll have another chance.'

'Yeh-yeh. You bet.'

Tiger finished his ministrations. 'Now you lie back an' take it easy. I'll bring yuh some chow up.'

Although the old ex-pug was a kind of rough handler he certainly had the bedside manner. He propped his patient up with pillows and lit a quirly for him before he left the room.

Bancroft sat thinking. It seemed it was now open war between him and the 'unofficial mayor' and his mob. Tiger was on his side, that was certain. So would Pete Otson be, but he was temporarily out of action. Bancroft figured Perce Maddison was on his side too, but, in his position, he didn't have to be too open about it.

Bancroft grinned crookedly. Why must he always be walking into trouble? Why should he be at war with these people? It all started because he brought in the body of an old man who'd been dry-gulched. He could light out tomorrow if he wanted to. But he wouldn't. This town was getting to be kind of interesting.

Anyway, he didn't like being pushed around by people who thought they owned creation. This train of thought led him inevitably to Burt Burgoyne. He'd met the old man's daughter. Now he'd like to meet the old man – he wouldn't mind meeting his daughter again either!

Well, he'd wait and see what the morrow brought.

He shouldn't have wondered. The four miscreants got off with a caution from Judge Gorter and a fine of five dollars apiece – which no doubt Mr Calhoun was glad to pay.

An apologetic sheriff visited Bancroft and told him there was nothing he could do about it.

'No, I guess not, Perce,' said the lean man.

Maybe Maddison's caution and tact was the best way after all. A man couldn't do much on his lonesome.

FIVE

The day after the mêlée in Tiger Macintosh's, Doc Penders visited Bancroft. The lean man's knee was swollen badly. Pender prescribed hot fomentations.

'Should do the trick in a couple of days,' he said. 'Then you can get out and about again. This time try to keep out of trouble.'

'Is that an order, Doc?'

Pender grimaced. 'I wish it were. But I guess you don't take orders. Anyway, I shouldn't like to see you carried out of town on a shutter. Some of the people here play for keeps if you force their hand.'

'Is that a warning, Doc?'

'Maybe. I still keep a whole scalp here because I'm the only doctor for fifteen miles, and they have to depend on me when they're sick. You're a stranger, and you're not a doctor. Watch yourself.'

'Thanks, Doc.'

'All right – see you again in a couple of days.'

'I'll come down to see *you*.'

'Yeh! Do that.'

Bancroft looked reflectively at the door as it closed behind the medico. A potential ally? Maybe!

A little later Tiger came in, and Bancroft told him what the doctor had said. The ex-pug's eyes glistened. The thought of hot fomentations intrigued him. But before he went downstairs again to concoct one, he had some news to tell the man on the bed.

'It seems the sheriff's bin down to the Buckeye Bar an' laid the law down to Calhoun. Told him he isn't so high an' mighty; that he could get him run outa town if he liked. Seems that ol' Burt Burgoyne holds a mortgage on the Buckeye Bar. I allus figured it belonged to Calhoun, but it seems ol' Burt's got a piece of it too – probably the biggest.'

'Has he got a piece o' this place, Tiger?' said Bancroft softly.

The other man snorted. 'Nope. Although he's tried. I threatened to throw Kit Hamden out on his ear next time he showed his face. He ain't since.'

'Good for you, Tiger. It seems ol' Burgoyne owns most o' the property round here, don't he?'

'I guess so. It's hard to know where he ain't got his fingers.'

'By fair means or foul?'

Tiger was uncertain. 'I dunno, I've never heard of him getting anything by foul means. He suttinly offered me a good price. He seems a strait-laced ol' galoot. Maybe he's jest got a mania for land and property. But that Kit Hamden – I wouldn't trust him. Maybe he does dirty tricks behind the ol' man's back. I'm suttinly lookin' out for 'em where he's concerned.

'Yeh, he's got all the makin's of a first-class sidewinder,' said Bancroft.

'This is how I figure it,' said Tiger. 'Hamden's purty thick with Miriam Burgoyne. He hopes to marry her. She'll inherit the Curly W an' he'll be master. I guess he figures it's good business tuh grab all the land an' property he can – under the ol' man's name now – hopin' it'll all come to him eventually. Why, he'd be the big boss around here – an' folks like me an' you'd be very small fry indeed. Right now, folks like me an' you stand in his way. No wonder he hates us like pizen.'

'Yeh.' Bancroft was still laconic. He was thoughtful for a few moments, then he said:

'Yuh know, what got me mixed up with this town in the first place was the murder of old Uncle Jeb.'

'Yeh.'

'Wal, yuh don't figure Hamden or any o' the Curly bunch had anything to do with that, do yuh?'

'Could o' bin lots o' folks around here done that. Ol' Jeb must've had a pile with him – an' maybe a map.'

'There wasn't a map on him when I found him.'

'No-o – I guess Jeb wouldn't carry one. He wuz smart – he'd keep it all in his noddle.'

'Looks like all this speculatin' is gettin' us no place at all,' said Bancroft. 'I guess if I'm gonna concentrate on tryin' tuh find out who killed Jeb I'd best jest fergit Hamden. One thing at a time. An' I suttinly do want to find out who killed Jeb. A certain section o' the community are doing their damnedest to pin it on me.'

'You jest take it easy, pardner,' said Tiger. 'Yuh cain't do no more roaring around for a few days, so jest rest up an' quit fretting – I'll jest go downstairs and git some o' them hot jiggers the doc spoke about.'

'I wuz afraid o' that,' said Bancroft with a wry grin. 'I wuz jest tryin' to put it off a mite.'

'No more,' said Tiger, and with a wide, almost threatening grin, went downstairs.

Bancroft lay and smoked and, despite Tiger's injunctions, kept on thinking.

The ex-pug returned gleefully with a steaming bowl of water and plenty of bandages, cotton-wool and towelling. Bancroft groaned aloud. 'Coupla days o' this an' I'll *have* to get up.'

The knee was stubborn, but after steaming like a volcano four times a day for the next three days, while Tiger gloated over it like a medieval sorcerer, it began to mend. On the fourth day Bancroft ventured forth into the hostile streets of Elkanville. His limp was more pronounced, but he felt fit. And pretty sure of himself.

He made straight for Calamity Kate's. He wanted to see deputy Pete Otson, who, according to Doc Penders, was on the mend and raring to go. Up till now Sheriff Maddison had got nowhere with his investigations. Maybe he was still too busy sparking Miriam Burgoyne. Not that you could blame him – he certainly had some heavy odds against him, by all accounts.

Kate greeted Bancroft with a grip like a Mississippi stoker.

'How yuh feelin', feller?'

'Fine, thanks.'

'You suttinly livened the town up, boy.'

'Trouble follers me,' said Bancroft modestly. 'How's the patient?'

'Fine an' dandy,' said Kate. 'He's bin askin' about yuh. Fine pair you are.' She laughed throatily. 'I guess soon as you're both fit you'll go out an' get shot up all over again. Go on up.'

Otson was sitting up in bed reading a news-sheet. He chortled aloud on seeing Bancroft.

'Wal, wal,' he said. 'So the ol' son-of-a-gun's hoppin' round again.'

'Shore thing,' said Bancroft. 'How's the wing?'

'Oh, fine. I wuz jest thinkin' o' gettin' up. I suttinly will now you're around again. Two's better'n one if there's another ruckas. An' I'm still a deppity lawman, yuh know.'

'You cain't do much with a gammy gun-arm.'

'Cain't I?' said Otson.

He swung himself out of bed. 'I bin up before, yuh know. Quite a bit. But I ain't bin outside. I bin kinda practisin'.'

'Practisin' what?'

The long redhead leered as he climbed into his trousers. With studied elaboration he pulled on his boots, put on his vest, tied his neckerchief, buckled on his gunbelt. All with one hand. Bancroft didn't offer to help him. He knew his man. Otson didn't need any help.

With his left hand, the deputy reached for a black silk scarf that hung on the bedrail.

'Doc says I gotta wear a sling for a mite yet,' he said. 'If he sees me without it he'll chew my ears off.'

He stood erect, his wounded shoulder and right arm in the sling, his left hanging at his side. His gun was in its usual place, the sheath strapped to his right thigh by a whangstring. Bancroft noticed, however, that the sheath and gun were turned around: the gun-butt was at the front instead of the back.

Otson grinned. His left hand swept across his belly, the gun snapped into his hand and was levelled at the other man's chest. Bancroft's eyebrows raised a little. It was the nearest his hard poker-face could get to surprise. That was the neatest bit of cross-arm drawing he had seen for a long time. Otson reholstered the gun.

'When I wuz a kid of seventeen or eighteen, up in Oregon during the Injun troubles, I got my right arm busted by an arrow. I've got the scar now,' said the deputy. 'My ol' man taught me that draw.' His voice softened a little. 'He was a grand ol' guy. He died fightin' Injuns. When they found him he had a ring o' the varmints – all dead – all around him. Thirteen of 'em. They ambushed him while he wuz out ridin'. He bedded down with his ol' buffalo gun. The Happy Huntin' Grounds suttinly received some guests that day.' Otson paused for a moment. Then he grinned and said: 'I bin practisin' that draw up here, quiet and private-like.'

'You suttinly ain't wasted your time,' Bancroft told him. 'That wuz plumb artistic. I ain't aiming tuh pick a fight with yuh.'

'Who d'yuh think you're kiddin',' said Otson. 'Maddison tells me you let Kit Hamden get his gun out, then beat him an' shot it out of his hand. An' Hamden's fast.'

'I guess Perce exaggerated a mite,' said Bancroft.

'Maybe,' said the deputy, but he didn't sound convinced. 'You know, Gimpy, Perce seems mighty proud o' you. Although he's kinda slow an' cautious-like, I guess maybe he'd like to be more like you. Y'know, he can spit when he wants to – but it suttinly takes a lot to get him goin'.'

'Maybe his way's the best.'

'Yeh, maybe, but I'd rather take chances now an' then. I guess he's just a big, easy-going, good-natured cuss, an' we gotta put up with him that way.'

44

Bancroft produced the 'makings' and rolled a couple of cigarettes. He handed one to Otson. They lit up.

Heels tapped on the stairs, halted outside the door. Came a knock.

'Come in,' said Otson.

The door opened. Miriam Burgoyne stepped into the room.

'Hello, Pete. How are you?' she said.

Otson opened his mouth and said: 'Fine, Miss Miriam,' and didn't bother to close it again.

She said: 'I only got back from Austin last night. Perce Maddison told me you'd been shot. I came as soon as I could. Dad sends his condolences.'

Otson had recovered his poise. He closed his mouth and smiled. 'I ain't daid yet, Miss Miriam.'

While the other two were talking, and as Miriam hadn't got around to noticing him, Bancroft had a chance to look her over.

She had removed her hat, and those reddish-golden curls that had caught his eye on a previous occasion were loose in all their shimmering wealth. The face below them was handsome, attractively bronzed, the nose rather arrogant, the lips rather scornful. The blue eyes were alive and fine. She was clad – for the day was hot – in a white shirt-waist, open at the neck to reveal her plump, firm throat. And a tweed skirt and riding boots. Her figure was shapely, but boyish rather than flamboyantly feminine. She was good to look upon, and Bancroft noted the broad shoulders, the firm, high breasts. Then she turned and caught him looking at her. Bancroft was too seasoned by climate and experience to blush, but he certainty felt like it.

Pete Otson said: 'This is Don Bancroft, Perce's old

pardner, Miss Miriam.'

'I saw Mr Bancroft once before,' said the girl. 'I've also heard quite a few conflicting reports about him.'

She held out her hand. As she gave his a firm clasp, Bancroft figured he knew where the conflicting reports came from. Perce Maddison had been rooting for him, and Kit Hamden just the opposite.

'Howdy, Miss,' he said.

The girl said: 'It's much more satisfying to be formally introduced.' Her blue eyes appraised him, then she gave a little ripple of laughter. 'I'm very relieved to find you do not sport a pair of horns and a tail, Mr Bancroft.'

Her eyes travelled downwards to the twin Colts strapped to his hips. She did not make any further remarks, but Bancroft gathered that she figured he did wear horns after all – though pretty low ones.

She turned again to Otson. 'I've an appointment with the milliner down the street, so I'll have to go. Look after yourself, Pete. And you, Mr Bancroft.'

She shot the latter a last quick, vital glance. Then she went. But she returned to pop her head around the door and say: 'I left a present downstairs for you, Pete. Something I thought you might need.'

'Thanks, Miss Miriam. So-long.'

' So-long,' echoed Bancroft.

'What a gal,' said Otson.

'Yeh,' agreed the other. 'I must say I was favourably impressed by the young lady. She wasn't so high-hat as I expected.'

'She can be,' the deputy told him. 'C'mon, let's go downstairs and look at her present. I haven't a clue what it might be.'

They questioned Kate, and after quite an amount of unladylike guffawing, she produced Miriam's present – a quart bottle of the finest whiskey. Otson took it as if it were a new-born babe.

'My,' he said. 'Who'd o' thought it.' Then again: 'What a gal!'

CHAPTER SIX

'We'll have a couple for the road,' Otson continued. 'To fortify us for our venture into the wide open spaces after our enforced bondage.'

'Hark at him,' guffawed Kate, her huge shoulders shaking, her bosom heaving.

'Glasses, Kate,' said Otson. 'An' don't forget one for yourself.'

'You shore can count me in,' she said.

She produced the glasses. Otson broached the bottle with the air of a connoisseur and filled each glass carefully to the brim.

They were emptied and filled again. And again.

When the two men finally left Calamity's joint the harsh tones of its proprietress, her voice raised in a mournful cowboy lament, floated after them. The men were seasoned drinkers. They were steady, but slightly lit-up, game for a joke or a fight.

As they passed the Buckeye Bar a big man came out on the boardwalk, saw them, paused uncertainly, then went back through the batwings. It was Big Lou.

Otson wagged his ginger head dismally from side to side.

'Pity,' he said. 'I'd've loved to practise my cross-arm draw on thet big galoot.'

But Bancroft's mind was busy with other matters.

He said: 'I can't figger that gal. What can she see in a snake like Kit Hamden.'

Otson simpered in a parody of femininity. 'Kit can be very charming at times.' His voice became dry. 'He's probably the little white-haired boy out at the ranch. He's good-lookin' an' a smooth talker. I gotta confess, Gimpy, I useter kinda like him myself until his overbearin' ways got my goat. Seems to me he's always posing when he's in town. Tryin' tuh show himself off as king o' the dungheap.'

'A gal who brings an ol' soaker like you a bottle o' whiskey when he's sick shore must understand men more than's ordinary.'

'Yeh,' said Otson. 'There's Maddison though. Maybe Miriam favours him all along. Then again – maybe she favours Hamden 'cos he's the arrogant type like herself.'

'Nothin' arrogant about her this morning.'

'Nope,' then Otson grinned. 'You're frettin' yourself to a shadow, Gimpy. C'mon, let's get somep'n tuh eat.'

They went into Tiger Macintosh's. The ex-pug greeted his returning boy with a half-anxious grin.

'Still all in one piece then,' he said. 'An' you, Pete, the doc ain't sawed your arm off.'

'Nope,' replied the deputy. 'He wanted to, but I talked him out of it. How 'bout you. How's the cranium?'

'Not a mark,' said Tiger. 'What grieves me is that the bottle he hit me with was half full of whiskey.'

'Quit your kiddin' an' get us some eats.'

'Right, gents. Sit yuhselves down.'

Olson and Bancroft crossed the floor to an empty table

against the wall. A few diners spoke to them. Others seemed uncertain and looked the other way or kept their mouths shut. Tiger advanced with the food, two piping hot plates of eggs, steak and baked potatoes.

'Coffee in a moment, gents,' he said. He bowed ironically and left them.

As they attacked the food the street door swung open again. Both men looked up. Three-ton Thurston, the undertaker, strode in. He paused a moment on the threshold, mopping his face with a red bandanna as his little eyes in their pouched fat surveyed the room.

I wonder whose side he's on, thought Bancroft. It irked him to be thinking now of everybody in terms of friend or enemy – but in circumstances such as he found in Elkanville he figured he couldn't do much else if he wanted to keep a whole skin. And there might even be enemies posing as friends – he hadn't thought of that factor until just now.

The huge undertaker's scrutiny was slow and deliberate. The townsfolk were used to it, many jokingly said he was sizing them up for future reference.

Finally his eyes alighted on Bancroft and the deputy. He crossed over to them and stuck out his huge paw. He shook them both by the hands and inquired gravely after their health.

'You ain't gonna get a chance to measure us up yet, Three-ton,' said Otson.

Tiger came with the coffee. 'Bring the usual over here, Tiger,' Thurston told him.

As Tiger went away the fat man turned again to Otson. 'Any idea who shot at yuh yet, Pete?' he said.

'Nope.'

'What's the sheriff doin' about it?'

'He's trailin' around, I guess. He cain't do much on his lonesome.'

Thurston grunted. He took out a thin black cheroot.

The three men became silent, Bancroft and Otson eating while Thurston blew out clouds of thick black smoke from the pungent weed.

The cheroot was half-smoked when Tiger returned with his food. Thurston dropped the smoking ember at his feet and crunched it beneath a huge heel. He attacked the food voraciously, oblivious now of everything else, smacking his fleshy lips with enjoyment as he crammed huge mouthfuls between them. Tiger brought coffee, and he swigged the cupful, steaming hot though it was. He asked for some more and another hunk of steak with fried potatoes to go with it.

But he was destined never to finish this, for, even as Tiger placed it under his nose, the door burst open and Pinky, the lanky, freckled assistant, burst in.

'Boss,' he said. 'We got a customer.'

'Crude boy,' said Thurston through a mouthful of food. 'I gather you mean somebody's dead.'

'Yeh – shot – down at the Buckeye Bar.'

Thurston lumbered to his feet. He sighed gustily. 'Wal, business is business. Lead the way, Pinky my boy.'

'We'll come along with you,' said Otson.

The little cavalcade filed out. Many of the diners had heard Pinky's words. They trailed along behind.

'Who is the deceased?' asked Thurston.

'Shorty Matthews,' Pinky told him.

Bancroft listened. He remembered Shorty. He was the little Curly W man who had fetched Maddison that time

51

just after Bancroft blew into town.

'Who shot him?' asked Thurston.

'The sheriff!'

Bancroft and the deputy exchanged surprised glances. That was certainly something, Maddison on the prod. This needed looking into. Killing a Burgoyne man, too! What had come over him?

They streamed through the swinging batwings of the Buckeye Bar. The place was packed with jabbering humanity. Pinky stepped aside and let his boss lead the way. Thurston churned through the mob like a tugboat, with a head of steam, through sluggish waters. The others followed in his wake.

They broke their way into a clear space against the bar where, looking up at them with wide accusing eyes, his head on the brass rail, lay Shorty Matthews. The front of his checked shirt was already saturated with seeping blood. Against the bar with his back to the room was Doc Ponders.

He was just fastening his bag. Beside him, half-turning, was Sheriff Maddison. He turned right around as Thurston advanced.

The undertaker ignored him and went down on his knees by his charge.

'He's makin' a mess,' he said. 'We'd best get him out of here.'

The hardened Pinky shook his head from side to side in mock disgust. Now the boss was being crude.

Thurston looked up. 'Can we take him away, Doc?' he said.

'Yes, take him away. I'll see tuh the rest.'

'Grab hold, Pinky.'

The crowd gave way again as the man and the youth,

with their grizzly burden passed through and into the sunshine. After that silent presence was gone, the chattering broke out with more animation. Bancroft and Otson moved up alongside the doctor and the sheriff.

'How'd it happen, Perce?' said Otson.

The sheriff was as phlegmatic as ever. His handsome face was set, his blonde hair glinted in the sunbeams coming through a small window beside the bar. He moved away from the bar and faced the other two, broad, straddle-legged, his thumb hooked in his gunbelt. He shrugged. He said:

'He spoke outa turn an' I hit him. He drew first and fired.'

He held out his arm, indicating the sleeve at the elbow. They saw the hole slightly brown at the edges where the bullet had passed through.

'He was purty close' said Bancroft.

'He was,' said Maddison. The slug from his own heavy Colt must have caved Shorty's ribs in.

The ranks of the crowd split again. Mike Calhoun came forth to confront the sheriff. He had been riding, the dust of the trail was still thick upon his boots. He looked wild.

He said: 'They tell me you killed Shorty.'

'That's right, Mike,' said Maddison. 'He throwed down on me, and I had to kill him.' He seemed the old mild Maddison once more.

The little tubby man seemed to puff up more with rage. His face contorted, he indicated the silver star on Maddison's vest with a wave of his hand, 'An' I suppose you wore your little badge nice an' prominent while you shot him, Mr Sheriff.'

'Shorty asked fer it,' said somebody in the crowd. 'Yeh, he shore did' . . . 'He drew fast' . . . The sheriff had plenty of backers.

Calhoun turned on them, snarling. 'Don't railroad me. I heard all about it 'fore I came in. The sheriff struck the first blow. An' why?' He turned once more to Maddison, leering. 'Because Shorty made a little harmless joke about the sheriff's lady-love – or at least the one he hopes to make his lady-love.'

Maddison went white around the lips. 'Don't ride me, Mike,' he said.

The saloon owner spat dryly, swivelled on his heels and passed through the trap in the bar into his private quarters. Maddison turned to the others. 'Shorty was a pard of his,' he said, as if excusing the tubby man.

It was later, when the sheriff had gone to report the killing to Judge Gorter, that Bancroft and Otson went to the undertaking parlour and got an eye witness account of the shooting from Pinky.

The youth began by saying: 'Wal, I saw it happen, but I don't rightly know how it happened.'

'Come again,' said deputy Otson.

'Wal – yuh see, the sheriff was sittin' havin' a drink with Shorty at one o' them tables right near the bar. Shorty wuz there first on his lonesome. Then Maddison came up tuh the bar an' got a drink, an' took it across tuh Shorty's table.'

'Go on,' said Bancroft. 'You've told us plumb nothin' yet.'

'Wal, although the place wuz purty full there wasn't nobody right near them, yuh see. I wuz over against the wall playin' cards with Copper from the livery stable.

Everybody was chattin' an' drinkin', an' gamblin' an' mindin' their own business.'

'Yeh.'

'All of a sudden the sheriff stands up an' Shorty stands up. Then the sheriff hits Shorty. His chair goes a-flyin', and he skithers down against the bar. He gets up sorta slow an' dazed-like, actin' as if he's gonna do nothin' about it. The sheriff seems to be sorta turnin' away, when Shorty livens up suddenly and draws. The sheriff steps on one side, but it's a near one. He's drawin' himself an' he shoots an' gets Shorty plumb centre. Shorty jest crumples up where he's standin' an' drapes himself across the brass rail.'

'Shorty asked for it then?'

'Yeh, I guess so. Although he wouldn't o' been much good against the sheriff in a fist-fight – a little cuss like him. I guess he wuz entitled to draw. He meant to kill the sheriff, I guess. It'd gotta be one of 'em.'

'Wal, what made Maddison hit Shorty in the first place? We know he spoke outa turn, but what did he say?'

'There wuz nobody near enough to hear anythin' properly, but one or two folks near said they thought they heard Shorty mention Miriam Burgoyne. An' jest after that Maddison hit him. O' course, that may be only rumour. I cain't figure how anybody could hear anythin' at all. Everybody was jabbering. You know how it is in there.'

'I guess Shorty must've said somethin' purty bad about Miriam,' said Otson. 'That'd be about the only thing that'd get Perce's goat. He wouldn't want to kill Shorty for it, though. I guess he jest had to.'

'Shorty allus was a poisonous little cuss anyway,' said Pinky.

SEVEN

The sheriff hadn't returned so Otson and Bancroft rode out of town. They took the trail to the foothills 'jest for a constitutional' as Otson put it, but, almost instinctively they steered their mounts through the narrow defile in the rocks to the place where they had been bushwhacked. They traced back from there to where they figured the bushwhacker might've been hidden. They found the place all right, back of a huge boulder. There were the marks of bootheels and a couple of cigarette stubs.

Bancroft fingered one of these. 'Hand-rolled,' he said.

'Most folks hand-roll their quirlies around here,' said Otson. 'The only place you can get the ready-made ones is in Austin.'

'Wait a minute,' said Bancroft. He had picked up another stub. 'This one looks like it's ready made.'

Otson took it. 'Shore does. Queer tho' to find a man smokin' both like this.'

'Maybe there was more than one man,' said Bancroft. Then he frowned. 'Though I only saw one high-tailing it. Maybe his buddy was still in hidin'. If so, he could've picked me off like a clay pigeon. Why didn't he?'

He gave a gesture of impatience. 'Aw, I'm jest blowin'.

It all gets us nowhere.' He went down on his haunches. 'The way the ground's scuffled about you can't tell whether there was one man, two, or a durned regiment.'

Otson grinned. 'Don't let it throw yuh, pard.' Then he said: 'I'd like tuh see where ol' Jeb got shot.'

'All right. I'll take yuh there.' They remounted and cantered back through the defile. Otson grimaced as they passed the place where he had lain. 'Shore didn't know what hit me!'

The sparse grass petered out altogether and then they were on the desert.

Bancroft reined in his horse and shaded his eyes.

'Now let me see. I was comin' from that direction when I saw the buzzards.' He pointed. 'I figure we'd better go this way.' He turned his horse's head a fraction. They rode on.

They drew further away from the foothills. Bancroft halted once more and looked back.

'It wuz later than this,' he said. 'So them hills wouldn't be so plain. I guess we're nearly there. Keep your eyes peeled for the carcasses of the burro and the horse. They're picked clean now I guess.'

'What's that?' Otson pointed.

It proved, however, to be only a clump of stunted cacti. They rode on slowly, looking about them, shading their eyes with their hands and squinting against the sun-glare.

'I think I see 'em,' said Bancroft.

He kneed his horse forward. Otson followed.

They came upon the skeletons of the two luckless beasts. The bones had been picked clean by the buzzards and bleached by the sun until they shone dully. The drifting sand had piled up against them; they were half-buried.

57

The ground around was dry and marked only by wind ripples.

Bancroft laughed sardonically as he looked about him. 'No use lookin' for clues around here,' he said. 'If the killer dropped his hat the sand would've buried it by now.'

'You'd 've seen it the first time anyway,' said Otson.

'Yeh.'

Otson said: 'Not a speck o' cover. The killer must've rode right up to the ol' man. It must've bin somebody Uncle Jeb knew. I cain't imagine that old-timer lettin' a stranger get within shootin' range.'

Bancroft showed more interest. 'Yeh, yuh got somethin' there. Not havin' known ol' Jeb I didn't think o' that.'

'I knew Jeb. He wuz a cagey ol' cuss.' Otson spat. 'Yeh, some *hombre* who Jeb figured wuz his pard – somebody he knew well – got the drop on him.' The deputy's voice became thick. 'I wish I'd got the skunk here.'

'Yeh,' said Bancroft. 'Wal, I guess we'd better mosey back. Maybe somethin'll sorta turn up.'

'Glad you're becoming a mite more philosophical,' said Otson, as he followed him.

Bancroft turned in his saddle and raised his eyebrows. Then he rowelled his horse to a gallop. Riding more carefully because of his wounded shoulder the deputy set his own mount after him.

They had passed through the hills and were back on the trail to town when Otson, who was still behind, turned and saw the horses and buggy coming up behind them.

'Slow down, Gimpy!' he yelled. 'We're bein' tailed.'

Bancroft obeyed and let the deputy catch up with him. They slowed to a jog-trot.

Looking back again Otson said: 'They're ketchin'-up.'

The next time he turned he gave an explosive exclamation. 'By all that's holy! It's ol' Burt Burgoyne. Miriam's drivin' him. I guess they've seen who we are by now. We'd better wait for 'em.'

The two men pulled their horses into the side of the trail. The buggy, drawn by two magnificent chestnuts, drew abreast of them and stopped in a cloud of dust. Miriam Burgoyne, unsmiling, looked imperiously down from her high seat.

The two ignorant waddies doffed their hats like little gentlemen and received a cold nod in return. This was the Miriam Burgoyne, the high-an'-mighty Miss Burgoyne, Bancroft had seen on his first night in Elkanville. So different from the laughing girl who had brought a bottle of the best hooch as a gift for a sick lawman.

The old man beside her did not even deign to nod. He simply glowered as if he would throw his feeble frame upon them. Bancroft wondered why the hell they had bothered to stop at all anyway. The road was clear wasn't it? Let them get to hell away from him. He didn't like being looked at as if he were some loathsome kind of lizard. He crammed his hat back on his head with unnecessary violence. Nevertheless he could not take his eyes off the personage who sat next to the girl.

The old man's white hair flowed out in a snowy floating mass from beneath the brim of a battered slouch hat. His thick walrus moustache was snow-white. It was not thick enough to hide the wide, grim, straight lips beneath it. His eyebrows were thick and very white, too, surmounting a pair of blue eyes that seemed almost to snap with life and passion. The old man's body was bent and thin. He was seventy, maybe more. But he had a pair of eyes like a trouble-shooting youngster. His features were grim, they looked as if they had been carved rather than modelled.

At the first sight of the old man's white hair Bancroft had thought about Santa Claus. But he stopped thinking that now. Burt Burgoyne looked every bit of what Sheriff Perce Maddison had called him – 'a real ol' fire-breathin' Puritan.'

Suddenly the rancher spoke. His voice, though not powerful, was resonant. He said: 'Who's your friend, Pete?'

'That's the Mr Don Bancroft I told you about, father,' the girl broke in.

'Hum,' said the old man. 'That right, Pete?'

'Yep, that's right, Mr Burgoyne.'

Bancroft scowled. All the big bugs of Elkanville seemed to figure they could jabber about him as if he were the little man who wasn't there.

He said harshly: 'I ain't deaf an' dumb, yuh know. I can talk. I even wriggle my ears sometimes.'

Burgoyne's features did not change expression as he replied: 'Wiggling your ears is a very innocent occupation. It causes no trouble. It harms no one. I wished you did nothing else but wiggle your ears, Mr Bancroft.'

'Every jackanapes in Elkanville would take me for a ride if that's all I did,' retorted Bancroft. 'When I'm pushed, I push back.'

Here the girl broke in. 'You pushed Kit Hamden pretty hard, didn't you?'

'He asked for it.'

'So Perce Maddison says. Still, maybe he's prejudiced.'

Otson broke in: 'Perce told the truth, Miss Miriam. Kit did ask for it.'

'Yeh,' said Bancroft. 'He acted as if he owned the town – and I had no place in it. He wasn't even polite.'

'He doesn't own the town,' said the old man. 'But I do.'

'Not all of it,' Bancroft told him.

'Some people are very stubborn,' continued Burgoyne imperturbably. 'They're liable to be more so if they think they've got a free-lance trouble-shooter siding with them.'

'Meaning me?'

'Maybe. I don't like trouble in my town, Mr Bancroft—'

'Not unless it's of your own makin' eh?'

'I don't make trouble. I try to avoid it. To have peace in this territory is my aim—'

'Even if it's a bloody peace! – I mean,' said Bancroft airily, 'you can't be responsible for what your men do.'

The old man leaned suddenly forward in his seat. His eyes were blazing, his face had paled. 'You rile me, Bancroft. I'll have—'

'Father,' the girl caught his arm. He leaned back in his seat. The girl looked down at Bancroft and her lips curled. 'You ruffian,' she said. 'I ought to've had more sense than to stop.'

The lean man smiled ruthlessly. 'The old man wanted to spiel, didn't he?' he said rudely. 'We didn't ask you to stop. Anyway, tell him it's as if I hadn't heard him.'

Miriam showed white teeth in a very unladylike snarl and raised the whip. Bancroft flinched as it stung his shoulder. Then she was lashing the horses, and they were away down the trail in a cloud of dust.

Bancroft looked after them, the queer little smile still on his face. He rubbed his shoulder.

'You suttinly got 'em both hoppin' mad,' said Otson. He looked worried. 'They'll have a rare ol' tale to tell the

61

sheriff when they get to town. Your name's gonna be pizen from now on. You'll hafta watch your step. Or blow alto-gether.'

'I wouldn't do that, Pete.'

'No. I guess not. I'd hate tuh see yuh go anyway. You must love being hated, old-timer.'

'Wal, I've bin hated in better places than Elkanville in my time.' Bancroft kneed his horse forward. 'C'mon, let's see what's cookin' up there.'

Otson followed him. He still wore a worried frown.

When they got into town it was the same as ever. Old Burt Burgoyne hadn't got a hanging-party waiting for Bancroft, or a sniper in every upstairs window.

'I guess the ol' goat an' the gal are closeted with the sheriff,' said Otson. 'What say you an' me go an' entertain Kate agin?'

'Suits me,' said the other, and they turned their horses towards Calamity's place.

Otson's guess at the whereabouts of the Burgoynes – father and daughter – had hit the jackpot. They were confronting a rather nervous Perce Maddison. Bancroft had been torn to pieces and thrown to the coyotes, and now the old man, getting down to what had really brought him there, was asking why in tarnation Perce had to shoot one of his best men. The sheriff looked from the old man to the girl. Then back again.

'He throwed down on me fust,' he said.

'But you hit him first, didn't you?' retorted the old man. Maddison wondered how in hell he'd got to know that so quickly.

'Yeh,' he said hesitantly. 'I guess I did.'

'Why, man? Why?'

'Well, I'll tell yuh,' said Maddison desperately. 'I haven't told anybody. I wuz savin' it for you. I'm purty sure now that Shorty killed ol' Jeb Carter – I confronted him with my suspicions an' he elected to treat 'em as a joke – a nasty joke,' he said. 'Then he made some remark about Miss Miriam an' I hit him—'

'Remark about Miriam? What remark?'

'I'd rather not repeat it, sir.'

'Well, what was the matter with him? Was he crazy? Why talk about Miriam when you'd just accused him of murder?'

'He was drunk, I guess.'

'He was a good man,' said Burgoyne thoughtfully. 'But nasty, I'll admit. Still, I couldn't think he'd kill old Jeb. What proof have you?'

'He had a coupla days off from work. The first day Jeb was killed. You sent him to fetch me. He'd jest rode in when you sent him, hadn't he?'

The old man was thoughtful. 'Yes, he had. He'd got two days comin' to him. That was the first one. I wondered what he was doin' hanging around on his day off. He said he'd just come in to get something, then he was going into town. Spike Thomas had jest rode in and told me Jeb had been murdered. He'd seen Bancroft bring him in. I told Shorty to send you to me as soon as he got in town.'

'Shorty wasn't in town long. He lit out an' he wasn't seen again in the district all the rest o' that day or the next. When he came back he seemed flush with money. He was flashing it about an' buying people drinks. I figure he must've ridden over the border and swapped ol' Jeb's gold for money.'

'Hum,' said the old man. 'He could have.' He snorted. 'But you haven't proven he did, have you?'

'No, not yet.'

'Well, you must then. Even though he's dead. You must make sure.'

'I will. But it'll take time. An' I might need more men. Them Mex's are mighty touchy o' American lawmen.'

'You can have the men. An' the time. Make sure of everything, that's all.'

'There was only a few bucks on him when Three-ton took him in,' said Maddison. 'He must've cached it some-where.'

'Find out if he did before you look for a cache,' said Burgoyne harshly.

'Yeh, yeh.'

The old man's blue eyes bored into him. 'You want it to be Shorty, don't you, Perce?' he said. 'So that friend o' yours, that Bancroft, will be in the clear. My money's on him rather than Shorty, Perce. I want him investigated, too. An' I want concrete proof if Shorty did it. Not just your sayso.'

'You ought to know you can trust me, Mr Burgoyne,' said the sheriff indignantly. 'I admit Gimpy Bancroft is an old friend of mine. But that doesn't mean he's not under suspicion. Still, he did bring the body in.'

'A smart move that!' said Burgoyne. 'He's a clever young man. I want to know what his game is.'

'He wuz jest passin' through, I guess.'

'For a man just passing through, he's certainly taking his time,' said Burgoyne dryly.

His chin sank on his chest. He seemed to be thinking deeply. The sheriff and the girl did not speak.

64

Suddenly the old man rose.

'I still wish you hadn't shot Shorty, Perce,' he said. 'Watch yourself—'

'I always do, Mr Burgoyne.'

'C'mon, Miriam.'

As they left, the sheriff shot the girl an eloquent glance, but received only a cool nod in reply.

The door closed behind them. The sheriff cursed between his teeth petulantly and drove his fist into the palm of his other hand.

He stood indecisive for a moment, then turned and sat in the chair at his desk. His handsome face was clouded. He picked up a pencil and scribbled absent-mindedly on a sheet of paper in front of him. He let up on this after a bit and began to tap on the desk with the pencil. He looked very worried. Suddenly, he rose, reached his hat from the hook behind him, and clapped it on his head. He crossed the room, then stopped dead and spun round on his heel. He retraced his steps, picked up his gun-belt from the bench where it had been slung, and put it on. Then he left the office, locking the door behind him.

He went first to Tiger Macintosh's place and accosted the bald-headed ex-pug as he was passing into the kitchen. 'Have yuh seen Bancroft an' Otson?'

'Not since this mornin', Perce.'

'Got any idea where they might be?'

'Nope.'

The sheriff looked a little uncertain for a moment. Then, without another word, he turned. Tiger shrugged and went on. Purty worryin', bein' a lawman in this town, he figured. He'd seen the two high-an'-mighty Burgoynes drive in, then out again. He guessed they'd been ridin' the sheriff. Perce looked like he wanted somebody's shoulder to cry on. He never ought to've been a lawman – he was too sensitive.

Unconscious of Tiger's almost sorrowing regard, Sheriff Maddison walked on down the street, his high heels thumping a rhythm on the boardwalk. He halted outside the Buckeye Bar. Somehow he didn't think the two men he sought would be in there. But he decided to make sure.

He parted the batwings and stepped inside. It was early for evening drinking, and the place was three-parts empty. The buzz of talk died down a little. Covert glances were shot at the lawman. What did he want in here again? Did it mean more trouble?

Some of the glances were truculent or malevolent. From certain sections there came angry mutterings as Maddison strode to the bar.

The barman eyed him uncertainly.

'Has my deputy an' his pard bin in here lately?'

The man shook his head. Then the peaceable Perce did a funny thing. Instead of turning and walking out, he said: 'Gimme a rye.'

The bartender hesitated, then he turned, grabbed a glass and a bottle and poured one out.

Maddison lifted it, took a couple of sips and replaced it on the bartop. He was not a hard-drinkin' man. His one foot on the brass-rail, his elbow on the bar, he was half-turned towards the room. He still looked worried and absent-minded. He did not seem to notice the hard glances that were thrown at him. Shorty Matthews had been pretty popular with the Buckeye Bar 'regulars.' Though a quarrelsome horny little cuss, he had been generous with his money when he was boozed.

'He's gotta nerve comin' in here after what's happened – even if he is a lawman.' This remark came from the back of the room, but it was loud and clear.

The sheriff did not seem to hear it. 'He's hidin' behind his little tin badge,' said somebody else.

Maddison turned his back and downed his drink.

A big man stood up at a table nearby. 'Ain't yuh gonna shoot anybody tonight, Sheriff?' he called.

Maddison turned and saw it was his and Bancroft's old enemy, Big Lou.

'I'm not in the habit o' comin' out tuh shoot people, you know that, Lou,' he said quietly.

For a moment the big man was nonplussed. Such smoothness always got him that way. He was a rough diamond and he didn't care who knew it. He scowled and came away from the table. Three other men nearby rose with him. Maddison recognized them as Calhoun men. Lou said:

'You killed Shorty, didn't yuh? He warn't doin' yuh no harm.'

'He drew first.'

Lou spat. 'You hazed him.' He came nearer. 'Take that durned star off,' he said.

'That's it! Don't hide behind your little tin badge, Sheriff,' shouted somebody.

Laughter greeted this sally. Here was sport. Very few of them there were on the sheriff's side. Even if they weren't friends of Shorty – even if they had nothing against Maddison personally, he represented the law. An' the law was pizen! People at the back rose to their feet and craned their necks as Lou and his colleagues moved nearer to the bar.

'Why don't you draw your gun an' shoot us all, Sheriff,' sneered the big fellow.

Maddison faced his tormentors, his back pressed against the bar, his elbows on its top.

'I'm here tuh keep the peace,' he said. 'But I warn yuh, Lou, don't press me too hard.'

Lou stopped walking. He threw back his head and guffawed.

'You ain't got Shorty now, Maddison,' he said. 'I call your bluff. Go ahead and draw.'

He stood with his arms dangling like a big ape. But his pardners sidled nearer.

'You'll get it first, Lou,' said Maddison. 'I can beat you, yuh know.'

'Can yuh?' Lou's little eyes shifted. He realized he'd put himself in a spot. Maybe Maddison could beat him at that.

He hadn't figured on any shooting, really, just to get near enough to knock the blond-haired boy around a bit. He figured Maddison, being the law, wouldn't draw first. He brought his hands up and out, a little away from his gun. He crouched a little and took a couple more steps forward.

'I warned yuh, Lou,' said the sheriff.

'You don't need no gun,' sneered Lou. 'Nor no tin star. I'm gonna beat the hades out of yuh.'

It was not Maddison's voice that answered this time, but another one from the back of the bar. It was a clear, melodious voice, and it said:

'Cut it out, Lou.'

The big man stopped dead again, his eyes swivelled. He stood erect, looking rather sheepish.

'Always wanting to beat somebody up,' said Mike

68

Calhoun. He was framed in the doorway of his office, to the left behind the bar. He was smiling. 'There are two things you must remember, Lou. Don't fight in my saloon. And don't pick bothers with big four-flushers wearing little tin stars. Little tin stars denote tinpot lawmen. You mustn't buck the law, Lou.'

Everybody laughed. Calhoun shore was a card! Lou grinned. 'Yeh, boss,' he said.

Maddison half-turned, looking at Calhoun. He smiled, too. Nothing seemed to be worrying him now.

'Thanks for callin' off the wolves, Mike,' he said.

Calhoun bowed mockingly. 'The pleasure's all mine, Mr Sheriff,' he said. 'I don't like my place messed up. Did you want to see me about something?'

'No. I'm goin' now.'

'All right,' said Calhoun. He shrugged.

Perce Maddison strolled to the door. He did not seem to hear the chuckles and sly remarks. He passed through into the night. Inside, somebody had said something funny. Everybody roared with laughter.

The sheriff walked down the street and turned into Calamity Kate's.

CHAPTER EIGHT

From the dark interior of what Kate was pleased to call 'The Lounge,' came the most gosh-awful sounds Perce Maddison had ever heard. If he had been walking into the dark maw of a cave peopled by Indian banshees he could not have expected worse.

However, after braving the wolves of the Buckeye Bar, he did not feel inclined to be hazed by a mere medley of weird noises. He plunged on through the ancient arched doorway and into the lounge. There was not a light on in the place.

The sound was louder now and seemed to come from the far end of the place by Kate's desk, which held the visitors' book. Maddison became sure that at least the noises were human.

'Hey!'

At this cry the wailing, for that was the only word Maddison could think of to describe it, abated a little. Then the sheriff distinctly heard a gruff voice say: 'Go jump in a crick.' After which the noise started up again with redoubled intensity.

'Pete!' bawled Maddison.

Some of the noises stopped. One single noise carried

on like the shrill, tortured shrieking of a rampaging norther, miles away but coming hell-for-leather across the range.

'Stow it, Kate,' said the gruff voice. 'The Emperor has arrived. Down on your knees, woman, an' bite his feet.'

'Aw, quit your pinchin',' squalled a female voice. 'You're spoiling my high notes.'

'Wal, if it ain't our li'l sheriff in person,' said another gruff voice. 'On the prod again, Percival?'

Everybody seemed to be having a sally at the law's expense tonight. Maddison recognized the sardonic tones of Gimpy Bancroft, a bit unsteadier than usual. He could see the three figures clustered round the desk now – and the bottles and glasses thereon. He went up to them, leaned against the desk with them.

The other two men were silent, but Kate kept up an agonizing warbling in a minor key.

'Cut it out, Kate,' said Bancroft. 'Say how-do-you-do tuh the nice sheriff.'

Deputy Otson leaned sideways until it seemed he would fall over, and looked owlishly into his chief's face. Maddison returned his look gravely.

'Hi-yuh, Pete,' he said, without warmth.

Pete straightened up. He wasn't as drunk as he pretended. He turned to Bancroft who was leaning against the desk. 'Somethin's eatin' the sheriff, Gimpy.'

'So,' said Gimpy curtly. He wasn't so drunk either.

'I'd like to talk to you boys,' said Maddison.

'Oh, Sheriff, who's gonna amuse Kate?' said Otson. Kate heard him and stopped catterwauling.

She leaned her huge body over from the other side of the desk and said mournfully: 'Don't you worry about pore

71

ol' Kate. Nobody worries about pore ol' Kate. Pore ol' Kate'll get along.' She began to chant in a tearful sing-song voice: ' Nobody cares f' pore ol' Kate—'

'Come on, boys,' said Maddison brusquely.

'Keep your shirt on, Perce,' said Bancroft.

Otson said: 'Let's go up to my room.'

The three men climbed the stairs, leaving Kate still moaning tearfully over the desk.

Maddison said: 'I just bin in the Buckeye Bar lookin' for you an' nearly got jumped by Big Lou an' some of his gang.'

'You might've known you wouldn't find us in there,' said Bancroft.

'How'd yuh make out,' asked Otson.

'Calhoun horned in an' stopped it. Everybody had a laugh at my expense . . . .' Maddison went on to tell the full story. He and Otson were seated on the bed, Bancroft on a chair by the window.

'You an' Calhoun useter be good pards,' said Otson.

'Yeh, he's only changed since Gimpy came. An' my run-in with Shorty really got him goin'. They wuz pals.'

'I'm a big worry tuh yuh, ain't I, Perce?' said Bancroft sardonically.

But the sheriff took the remark quite seriously. 'Yeh,' he said. 'Kinda.'

'Maybe I'd better ride.'

'Yeh, maybe.'

'But I guess, bein' an ornery, stubborn sort of cuss, I cain't until I know who killed ol' Jeb Carter.'

'I think I can tell you that. That's partly what I came after you for.'

'Did Papa Burgoyne tell yuh who done it?' said Bancroft.

'Cut it out, Gimpy,' said Otson.

Bancroft shrugged. Maddison did not look at him. He said: 'I'm pretty sure Shorty Matthews done the shootin'. I tackled him about it – that's why he tried to shut my mouth.'

'We heard you'd quarrelled over Miriam Burgoyne,' said Bancroft.

'Yeh, he did say somethin' about Miriam. That's when I hit him. He didn't seem tuh take my accusation seriously. He was drunk.'

'If you hadn't killed him, he might've talked.'

'Yeh,' agreed Maddison. 'I guess I shot too straight.' He sounded more amiable now.

'Have yuh got proof Shorty done it?' said Bancroft.

'No. But I think I can get it purty quick.'

'Wal,' said Bancroft, carelessly. 'When you've got it all cut and dried maybe I'll mosey along a piece. This place is kinda gettin' in my craw lately. I guess I could never be a courtier tuh the local king.'

'Oh, old Burt ain't so bad,' said Maddison. 'He likes his own way. I guess he's entitled to it. I kinda like the ol' buzzard although he bawled me out this afternoon.'

'Did he?'

'Yeh. He won't believe that Shorty killed ol' Jeb. He thinks you had somethin' tuh do with it.'

'Oh, he does, does he?'

'Yeh. An' he can make it very hot for you round here. He says even if you didn't have anythin' to do with Jeb's death you're a trouble-maker, an' he don't want trouble-makers in this town.'

'Oh, he did, did he?' said Bancroft, parrot-like. Maddison was either too stupid or too tactful to notice the

73

underlying mockery in Bancroft's voice. He said, rather haltingly:

'So I wondered if you'd jest mosey along for a week or so – until I've proved Shorty's guilt an' things have blown over. Then yuh could come back.'

'An' say if yuh don't prove Shorty's guilt – how do I stand then? Not very healthily I guess; the ol' man's bound to think I done it then.'

'Aw, Shorty's guilty right enough,' said Maddison. 'I'm jest tryin' tuh do the best all round.'

'Wal, Perce,' said Bancroft softly. 'I guess your best won't do for me. I'll leave this town when I'm good an' ready. An' you can tell your boss tuh go tuh hell. An' I'm tellin' yuh, Perce, as far as I'm concerned we're still pards – but don't none of yuh press me too hard, that's all.'

The sheriff had regained his usual composure. He shrugged. 'I'm sorry you feel that way about it, Gimpy. We're still pards sure. What brought yuh here in the first place?'

But Bancroft was not to be mollified. The last question made him scowl.

'Why didn't the ol' man ask me all these questions himself?' he said. 'He had the chance this afternoon.'

'It's nothin' tuh do with the old man. I gotta ask these questions.'

'Why didn't you ask 'em before then? You've seen enough of me since I've been in town.'

'I didn't think there was any need before. I'm jest tryin' tuh clear you that's all.'

'Aw hell.' Bancroft rose. 'Stop bein' so mealy mouthed. If you think I killed ol' Jeb – well – try an' take me in.'

He stood upright, his hands dangling.

Otson rose, too. 'What kinda fools' talk's this?' he said. 'Let's go for a walk to clear our heads.'

'I told him Shorty done it,' said Maddison.

'C'mon, let's go,' said Otson. 'C'mon, Gimpy.'

The lean man smiled mirthlessly and followed him to the door. The sheriff followed rather meekly.

'Hi-yuh boys,' Kate greeted them.

'Be back later, honey-bunch,' said Otson.

'What's the matter wi' them two buzzards,' said Kate. 'They look like they're goin' to a funeral.'

'I hope not,' said Otson softly. Only the men heard him.

The sheriff drew level with Bancroft as they got out on the boardwalk.

'I didn't mean tuh get your goat, Gimpy,' he said. He stuck out his hand.

Without a word Bancroft took it. They shook.

As the three men approached the Buckeye Bar they could see a bunch of people on the boardwalk in the rays of light from the swinging batwings. From inside came the roaring chorus of a song and the clankety-clang of a misused piano.

As they drew nearer a voice roared: 'Here comes that sheriff agin. An' he's got his pals with him this time.' It was Big Lou, and he was plenty drunk. There were about half-a-dozen men altogether, and Lou towered a head above all of them.

Guffaws of laughter followed Lou's sally. Then the men became silent, watching the others as they approached, their boot-heels beating a slow march on the boards.

Maddison said out of the corner of his mouth: 'They're blocking the way. We don't want any trouble.

We'd better step off on to the road.'

'D'yuh think that'll make any difference? Lou's raring tuh go – he evidently didn't like his boss tellin' him what's what in there tonight. Stepping on to the road won't keep him quiet.'

'I guess you're right, Gimpy,' said Pete Otson. 'I'm with yuh.'

'What's the matter with yuh, Perce?' said Bancroft. 'You're sheriff, ain't you?' He was in a truculent mood tonight. He felt like taking the town apart.

The sheriff did not answer him. But he did not step into the road either.

They neared the group, who began to chatter, awaiting their leader's cue. Big Lou was not slow in giving it. He said: 'Have you come back to settle our little argument, Sheriff?'

'I've told yuh before – I'm here tuh keep the peace,' said Maddison. 'Step aside, Lou.'

'We'd better rush 'em,' said Bancroft softly.

Lou stood directly in the sheriff's path. Both Otson and Bancroft discovered their ways were blocked. It was odds of six to three.

The deputy was the sparest of the three; maybe that was why two of the roughs opened up first by simultaneously attacking him. Otson kicked one on the shins, causing him to howl and caught the other's blow on his shoulder – not on his head for which it was intended. Bancroft slammed the nearest one to him plumb centre, doubling him up, following it up with a straight smack right between the eyes. That was one down for the count, one less to deal with.

Big Lou and Maddison were wrestling, they left the

sidewalk together, toppled and rolled in the mud. Very undignified for his friend, the sheriff, Bancroft thought sardonically, as he squared up to the next in line. Then he threw himself to one side just in time to avoid a viciously swung gun. Here was something he had not bargained for. Guns out made things ticklish. It only wanted somebody to press a trigger, on purpose or in the excitement of the moment, and this would speedily turn from an ordinary rough-house to bloody carnage. The man looked familiar. Bancroft figured he was one of those who had helped to beat him up in Tiger's place. Maybe he had caught a packet then and didn't want it to happen again.

He got in close and grappled the man, getting hold of his gun-wrist. The man used his knee. Bancroft winced. Driving his fist like a piston, driven by that sudden stab of pain, two sharp blows spattered in the middle of the man's face. He wilted. But Bancroft still held him, gun and all, and hit him again and again. Then he let him drop in a crumpled heap. The gun clattered to the boardwalk.

People were pouring out of the Buckeye Bar now. And most of them seemed hostile. The partners were in a tough spot.

Bancroft turned swiftly to see how Otson was faring. The deputy was up against the wall being slugged by a newcomer almost as big as Lou.

Bancroft thought and acted swiftly. He drew his gun and hit the big man on the head with it all in one swift motion. Then he yelled: 'Let's get goin'.'

He backed away on to the road, the gun dangling at his side. Otson followed him. The sheriff was on his feet. Big Lou was just rising. As he was half-crouched the sheriff drew back his foot and kicked him on the side of the

77

head. Maddison was seeing red again. He sure was a changeable man. Lou went flat on his face in the dust and lay still.

A low growl came from the crowd. Bancroft elevated his gun. 'Easy,' he said. 'We cain't fight all of yuh. I'll drill the first man who makes a false move.'

Both the sheriff and his deputy had their guns out now.

'You people are bein' steered wrong,' said Maddison. 'You know me. I play straight.'

'Maybe,' said somebody. 'But we don't like the company you keep.'

'Yuh can give a man a chance, cain't yuh,' retorted the sheriff. 'I'm law here, if I've got proof agin anybody I act on it. Till then I don't listen tuh idle talk and rumours. I shouldn't like to have to get me a bunch o' tough deputies to ramrod this town.'

Bancroft listened and speculated. Perce sure was telling 'em straight now. He began to be sorry for his earlier orneriness.

Somebody said: 'Lou looks like he's daid.'

'We're movin' on now,' said Maddison. 'Some of yuh better come an' have a look at him. But remember, all Lou got he asked for.'

'Let's mosey,' said Bancroft. 'But hold on to your guns.'

The sheriff seemed to be on the verge of reholstering his.

'You're too trustin', Perce,' Bancroft told him. So the sheriff kept it in his hand.

Watched by the uncertain crowd the three men backed away to the opposite side of the road. There in the shadows, they turned about, their eyes on the crowd, who now could only dimly see them but, silhouetted in the light, were good targets themselves. The three men still held on to their guns.

One intrepid *hombre* crossed to Big Lou. They let him. Others followed. The street became fairly well populated. Everybody chattered.

Above it all a gun boomed. Bancroft's hat spun from his head. The three men threw themselves back against the walls in the shadows.

'It came from the alley beside the Buckeye,' said Otson. 'Gimpy!'

But Bancroft was already half-way across the road.

'Hell!' said Otson. But he followed. Maddison brought up the rear.

Behind him, more from curiosity now than malicious intent, streamed others. The alley filled with people. They straggled around the back of the Buckeye Bar, disturbing prowling cats among the ashcans.

The sheriff and his deputy ran into Bancroft. He said: 'I think it's the same guy who pulled a gun on me durin' the fightin'. He's all likkered up.'

'Where is he?'

'I lost him. But he's back here somewhere. He didn't have time to get away.'

The temper of the crowd had changed now. Big Lou was still out cold on a bench inside the saloon, his bull-like tones could not egg them on to lawlessness and devilment. They prowled among the ashcans and rubbish-heaps that littered the yards, shouting and chattering, singing out from time to time for the bushwhackin' galoot to come out an' show himself.

Then suddenly all hell broke loose as shots blasted the night again. The revellers scattered. Bancroft plunged forward, gun ready. Otson followed him, lost him in the darkness. He turned. He couldn't see Maddison either. Guns were out all around. And they were popping, most of them pointed at the air, through sheer nervousness – and because their owners didn't know what to shoot at either.

The back door of the Buckeye Bar opened. A figure was silhouetted in the light that streamed out. The figure waved its arms and seemed to be shouting. It went. Then returned holding a shotgun.

The din made the night hideous, the blackness was stabbed with flame. Suddenly the figure swayed forward, away from the door. Then it disappeared.

Crouching, Pete Otson ran to the door. Outside it, in the darkness, a man lay. The shotgun rang musically as Pete kicked it. He went down on his knees by the still form, tried to lift it up. His hand became daubed with stickiness.

'Hell!' said Otson. Then he yelled at the pitch of his lungs. 'Sheriff! Sheriff! Somebody's been hurt.'

The noise did not abate, but already others had drawn near to the man on the ground and the kneeling deputy. The word passed around. Gradually, but finally, a silence fell.

The sheriff joined Otson and Bancroft, who had not caught his man.

Between them they carried the man inside. It was Mike Calhoun. He was still alive – just!

'Fetch Doc Pender somebody,' said Maddison harshly.

They carried the saloon keeper upstairs to his room and laid him on his bed. His face was white, almost baby-ish in repose, his eyes tight-closed. The wound was in his chest. His shirt was saturated, but he was not bleeding quite so much now.

Bancroft it was who dressed the wound, wadding it, and

binding it with clean white sheeting. 'He's got a chance,' he said. 'There ain't anythin' more we can do till the doc gets here.'

'Who could've fired the shot?' said Maddison. 'Either of you see?'

Neither of the other two had. 'I heard Pete shout an' I came a-running,' Maddison told them.

The sheriff and his deputy went downstairs to question others. Nobody knew anything. Some of them asked where Bancroft was. Their reactions on hearing that he was upstairs watching over Calhoun were varied.

'It's takin' the doc long enough,' said Maddison. 'Somebody went, didn't they?'

Just then they returned. Doc Pender was not at home. They had split up, four of them and scoured the town. They couldn't find him any place. Nobody had seen him lately.

Bancroft came down the stairs. Maddison looked up. 'They can't find the doc, Gimpy,' he said.

'He won't be needed now, anyway,' said the lean man tersely. 'Calhoun's dead.'

The announcement was greeted by dead silence which hung in the air for a moment like crystal, and then was rudely shattered by another voice which said clearly: 'Sheriff! Arrest that man!'

All heads swivelled. The crowd parted to let through Kit Hamden, the Burgoyne foreman, who strode towards the sheriff. But his eyes were fixed on the man who stood at the foot of the stairs. Bancroft returned his look, and in both pairs of dark eyes there was naked hate.

The sheriff did not seem pleased to see Hamden either. He said:

'What's bitin' yuh, Kit?'

The young foreman held the centre of the stage. He was very sure of himself. His dark face was arrogant, his voice level and resonant as he turned to the sheriff and said: 'Every time there's a shootin' this man,' he indicated Bancroft with a jerk of his head, 'is around. He brought ol' Jeb in. In my opinion, that was just colossal bluff. But you fell for it. When Otson was shot he was ridin' with him—'

The deputy chimed in. 'Use your head, Hamden. I was hit by a rifle slug, from a distance. Gimpy was right behind me—'

'He must be workin' with somebody else – somebody here, or somebody we haven't seen. Are yuh blind, or just plumb silly? Don't it strike you as queer that every time anybody's shot in mysterious circumstances this *hombre*'s around someplace?'

There were growls and murmurs from the listening crowd. Many of them evidently were on the arrogant Hamden's side for once.

The young foreman, like an actor playing to the gallery, turned round towards them.

'Can't you see that the sheriff is shielding this man because he's a friend of his—'

'Hold on, Hamden.' This from Maddison. 'You ain't got no proof—'

The dark young man ignored him.

'Nobody saw who shot Calhoun. I'm told this Bancroft *hombre* had run on alone. He could've potted Calhoun easy from the back there. It's my belief he shot ol' Jeb, got his pard to bushwhack Otson – that's why he wasn't hit himself. An' he shot Calhoun because he was the one who had accused him – who was untiring in trying to get justice done—' The crowd growled again.

'That's slander,' said the sheriff. 'You got no proof at all. You—'

'If I might be allowed to speak!' This voice cut in clearly through the general babble.

Bancroft still stood on the two bottom steps of the stairs, one foot above the other. He was lean and straight, and his face wore its usual sardonic expression. He seemed pretty cool. He was interrupted.

'What did yuh stay up there for, anyway?' Hamden shouted hotly. 'So's you could make sure Calhoun was daid.'

'How came you just busted in from nowhere yourself?' said Bancroft. 'Where've you bin skulking while all the fun's bin on?'

'I jest rode in tuh see Calhoun on business. I heard the news outside – all what happened. I came in. Dozens o' people here saw me ride in—'

He was backed up once more by voices in the crowd.

'You could've bin skulking round the back, shot Calhoun, got away, an' still come ridin' down the street as if you'd jest arrived in town.'

'There's somethin' in that,' said the sheriff.

'You'd like tuh believe that, wouldn't you, Perce?' sneered Hamden. 'You'd sooner pin it on me than on your pard here. I forgot tuh tell yuh, Perce, I got some more bad news for yuh. Your other little scapegoat ain't any more. Pore Shorty died fer nothin'. Them two days he wuz away when you reckoned he was saltin' ol' Jeb's haul over the border, he was up at a relative's home. The boss's got proof o' that. He comin' in again to see yuh personally about it.' He raised his voice, turning to the crowd again.

'I guess if Perce here don't buck up we'd better look for another sheriff. If he don't take this yere Bancroft in I will.'

Judging by the reception given to this stout resolution he would have plenty of helpers.

'Turn around, Hamden, I'm liable tuh shoot yuh in the back.' It was Bancroft's voice again. He had come away from the stairs now and stood, legs apart, thumbs hooked in belt. The Burgoyne ramrod turned to face him.

'Yuh know I c'n beat yuh, don't yuh, Hamden?' said the lean man. 'But if I did it'd be just another killin' agin me – an' this mob o' yourn 'ud probably tear me tuh pieces. So you know I won't shoot yuh. Maybe – that's what you're backin' on anyway. All right, come on. Come on and take me!'

For a fraction of time Hamden hesitated. Then he slowly unbuckled his gunbelt.

'I don't need guns to take you,' he said.

NINE

'Wal – if that's the way yuh want it,' said Bancroft. He, too, unbuckled his belt. Pete Otson went over and took it from his hands. It was a nice gesture on the deputy's part. It meant that the lean man still had at least one friend in the assemblage.

The crowd began to move back to give the contestants more room. Maddison stood uncertainly.

'Get out of the way, Sheriff,' said Hamden.

Still looking rather dazed by the sudden turn of events, Maddison let Otson pull him back to the front rank of spectators. There was silence now. The crowd waited. A good mill was better entertainment than any gun-fight, and lookers on weren't so liable to get hurt, either.

The two men stood looking at each other for a pregnant moment. Bancroft was the taller and the leaner. His dark, narrow face had not changed its sullen, half-mocking expression. Hamden was just as dark, a little shorter, but broader of build and younger. His face looked almost boyish and was set in hate and scorn. He was the first to move, advancing slowly towards his enemy.

Bancroft moved forward a couple of paces himself, his

arms dangling, his hands loose. Then he stopped and waited.

As Hamden got nearer, he brought his hands up, balled them into fists. He shaped well – like a bantam-cock, very sure of himself and raring to go. But wary, not underestimating his opponent. Bancroft looked too cool and too tough to be easy meat.

Hamden veered a little, dancing to the side. The crowd hummed, then was silent again. Not a blow struck yet! But the suspense was killing.

Bancroft turned to face the Burgoyne man. His own hands went up, the fists broken, bony and knotted. They sparred like fencers. Then swiftly, like tempered blades, they clashed.

Bancroft parried Hamden's blow and retaliated. His fist thudded on Hamden's shoulder.

The crowd began to yell. For a moment the din was hideous – a primeval, blood-lusting babble. Then it died down to a sibilant murmur as the fighters really began to settle down to a slogging match. They stood almost toe-to-toe now, elbows bent, fists driving, their shoulders squared with power.

Bancroft teetered on his heels as a terrific blow laid his cheek open. The murmur became a savage shout. First blood to Hamden!

But the young ramrod was over-eager. His follow-up blow missed entirely. He ran right into the lean man's fist and rebounded as if he had been kicked by a steer. He went over on his back, his legs kicking upwards. He rolled, catlike, and jumped to his feet. Bancroft swept in and hit him again with a chopping, sideways blow to the angle of the jaw. Hamden's gasp of agony followed the smack of the blow. He went down on his shoulder. Bancroft stepped back, watching him, his face expressionless.

Hamden rose on one knee, his one palm flat on the boards, his other hand fisted, ready to lunge. This reaction was almost mechanical; he still seemed dazed. His eyes sought Bancroft, focused. He straightened up and leapt all in one panther-like movement. All the weight of his stout body was behind that out-thrust right fist. It smashed through the lean man's guard and hit him flush on the temple. Then Bancroft was down and Hamden stood aside, his broad chest heaving, one side of his face crimson and already beginning to swell.

The fallen man's lean body uncoiled like a spring and as quickly spun, and Hamden rushed in, throwing blows from all angles. Although none of the blows connected with any force on the weaving Bancroft, Hamden's weight was forcing him backwards. The small of his back hit the sharp rim of a table and he was pulled up short. The young ramrod hit him square in the mouth. His head jerked back, then sideways, as he instinctively avoided the next blow. He retaliated to Hamden's body, cruelly punishing blows that doubled the youngster up. But did not stop him.

Bancroft slid away from the table. Hamden's rush carried him across it. He spun, spreadeagled. The table went over with a crash, one of its legs snapped off clean. The crowd moved out of the way that side-closed in on the other. The arena shifted.

Hands helped the Burgoyne man to his feet, propelled him back into the circle. The lean man advanced, stabbing with his left. Once, twice, three times. Hamden's head went back, his fists went up to stop this piston-like punishment. Bancroft's right rammed itself into his solar plexus. Hamden gasped and folded right into a terrific uppercut that lifted him off his feet and deposited him on his back with a dull thud.

Bancroft moved back jerkily. There was a half-smile on his bloodstained face. His eyes looked hard and merciless. Hamden lay flat beside an overturned chair. Nobody came forward to help him this time. He grasped the chair and slowly pulled himself to his feet. His face was a mess of blood from which his eyes blazed. He was game. But he was hurt, and he took his time drawing himself erect. He drew the sleeve of his shirt across his eyes, flung his hair back with an impatient gesture. Then he advanced on the motionless Bancroft.

The lean man waited, legs apart, hands dangling. The one gashed side of his face was a sorry sight. As Hamden came nearer his foot came forward, his hands moved up again, half-clenched. They came up higher, balled, blocked the ramrod's first two high blows. But Hamden followed up with his heavy body, his arms crossed in a 'smother' guard as Bancroft retaliated. Then the arms unfolded swiftly, lashing whiplike. Both fists caught Bancroft flush in the face. The lean man staggered. He was off-balance as Hamden's next blow, delivered with all his power, hit him again in the face. He was propelled across the room. The bar stopped him. He slid down to the brass rail. He clenched it with both hands, shaking his head furiously to dispel the fog. Then, still holding grimly to the brass foot-rail, he drew himself up to a sitting position.

Hamden stood, swaying slightly, in the middle of the floor. His face was out-thrust slightly, he wiped the blood from his eyes again with his sleeve. He peered at the fallen man.

He hitched up his belt with both hands, shrugged his broad shoulders, tried to steady himself as he saw the fallen man begin to rise slowly.

Bancroft had his hands on the bartop now and was straightening his long legs. Hamden began to advance, half-crouching, shoulders hunched a little. Bancroft faced him, his elbows on the bar, his back against it. From here he suddenly launched himself, his feet scraping the boards. Hamden met him.

The crowd went wild again. The front rank billowed like the surf on a shore, washing Otson and the sheriff with it. The former was watching the fight with avid interest. But Maddison's face was expressionless. He did not seem to know where he stood – how he stood.

The two men stood in the arena and beat at each other like tried gladiators. They stood almost toe to toe, and neither man gave an inch, although their bodies swayed and their heads jerked. It was Hamden who gave first, from one of Bancroft's cruel body blows. He doubled up and slid to his knees. Bancroft's *coup de grâce* merely brushed his hair. Then the lean man hauled off and stood still.

Even as he rose, Hamden launched himself forward, retaliating in kind by driving both his fists into Bancroft's midriff. Right there Bancroft hadn't got much that could be hit. But he folded up like a jack-knife. Hamden did not miss with his next one either. It was a terrific round-arm swing and caught the lean man on the side of his head. The sound it made was like the echo of a rifle-shot in a valley. Bancroft's boot-heels shrieked as he went along the floor to end up amid a pile of two chairs and a small table. Nothing in that pile was the right way up. But these boys were tougher than wild horses. Nobody was very much surprised to see the lean man's narrow head poke up like a turkey-cock's. Hamden wasn't surprised. He looked just a mite discouraged as he stood and waited, teetering on his heels a tiny bit.

Bancroft just shoved the table out of his way. He didn't feel steady enough to climb over it. His face was a bloody mask of pain. But his eyes were undimmed. He advanced to Hamden, crouching a little, his arms dangling like an ape. Then he leapt, his arms swinging, his fists cracking like gunshots as they landed on Hamden's face. It seemed the young ramrod was too tired to defend himself. But, as he staggered his arms automatically moved to block further blows.

Bancroft backed away. He was tired, too. He was almost tottering. Both men weaved and swayed, facing each other, getting a breather, waiting for that second strength that comes to all good fighters some time.

They joined up again, gradually this time, poking tentatively at each other like playful grizzlies. But, like grizzlies, they were still very dangerous. They were cunning, biding their time.

It was the youthful Hamden who opened up first. A straight left to Bancroft's already bulging lips was followed by an uppercut that only just misfired – lucky for the lean man. He slid away, his feet scraping sluggishly on the boards. Not fast, seemingly, but fast enough to fuddle Hamden for a moment. Then Bancroft slid in again, stooping, changing his tactics as he moved under Hamden's guard. But the youngster blocked the body-blows; previous ones had been a painful lesson; he knew he couldn't stand any more. Bancroft switched again and upper-cutted him, rocking him back on his heels.

Both men were calling in that reserve of strength now. A reserve made potent by the hard, healthy life they led, and by the fact that they were both born fighters.

The crowd were seeing something great, and they knew it. Something to write home about, something to tell around the camp-fire on a cold night, or in a bar for a drink when they were broke – or, if they lived to be old and horny, to their grandchildren gathered round them at the fireside. The oldtimers amongst them chewed their plugs, spat, cackled and clapped their hands. What a fight! What a fight! *Reminds me o' the time, Cal, when . . . Remember, Jake, when . . .* Then they'd quit talking, and watch, their old eyes sparkling with excitement and memories reborn as, like two young bulls locking horns, the fighters came together again. Fair, clean, beautiful, brutal.

Hamden whipped a right cross to Bancroft's jaw, a glancing blow that made the lean man wince. Bancroft threw a straight punch deep beneath the young ramrod's heart. It would have been a killing blow, but Hamden was backing away and he did not feel its full power. He swerved and bored in; punching simultaneously, both men connected with blows to the face, but so battered were they both now that they did not seem to feel them. For a moment it was a grand, terrible mix-up, each man giving all he'd got. And taking it, too, as if it were mere hailstones. They were robots now, fighting each other to a standstill. But, the old-timers said, men had been known to go on like that for hours.

The sheriff started forward as if he would try to stop

them, but Otson pulled him back. The sheriff still looked kind of dazed – though many affirmed spitefully that he never looked any different.

Furniture crashed over again as the contestants plunged from the arena and carried the fight towards the crowd, which swayed and moved again. Bancroft had Hamden across a table and was battering at him unmercifully with arms like flails, each swing jerking his own tired body forward as if it were stuffed with sawdust. The table went over and both men with it, now side by side, but turning to grapple each other. Doubtless all either of them felt now was the primeval desire to still the irritating pain-bringing creature that opposed him. But the gruelling battle was not yet over.

They rolled away from the table. Hamden rose and stood unsteadily, waiting for Bancroft. Then, as the latter straightened his lean body, Hamden swung at him. He only hit Bancroft's shoulder, but the blow deflected the one Bancroft had intended for the youngster's sorely bruised body. They fell against each other in a clinch, their arms pumping mechanically. Hamden received a terrible blow in the throat that felled him. The crowd hummed. The lean man was a deceptive customer: he'd still got more strength than anybody figured, including, it appeared, his opponent.

For a short, pregnant moment, while those at the back craned their necks and asked excited questions, it seemed Hamden was out for the count. But he was playing 'possum, getting a breather.

He jumped up with startling suddenness and sprang at Bancroft. The latter side-stepped but he wasn't fast enough; Hamden's heavy body hit him and spun him around. He hit a chair and instinctively clung to it. It held him for a split second, then tipped. He went down on his hands and knees. Hamden stood over him, teetering like a drunken man. Bancroft shook his head from side to side. He straightened up suddenly; then, as Hamden sprang again, bent his back. The Burgoyne man went clean over it and head-first into the crowd. They hauled him to his feet and pushed him forward again with would-be encouraging zeal. But it was misplaced. Bancroft dodged and, unable to stop himself, Hamden sprawled on his face. He rose more slowly. He was a horrible sight and he looked murderous. With a space of about four yards between them, the two men stood and looked at each other, each one conserving his strength, waiting for the other to move first. Bancroft's shirt had fallen out of his belt and was torn down one side. Red-checked, it hung on his lean body like a banner. He had rolled the sleeves back, but one of them had come loose and dangled, limp and torn, around his sinewy arm. As he stood there, he began to roll it up again slowly. His face was smothered with now-drying blood, the gash in his cheek looked sore and seemed to be having some effect on the eye that side. His lips were puffed but just managed to keep their sardonic curl. He finished fixing the sleeve and brushed back his lank brown hair with his hand. He stood, feet apart, leaning backwards a little, watching Hamden dispassionately.

In contrast, the young ramrod was crouched a little, a stance he had instinctively adopted to guard against the cruel body-blows Bancroft was so fond of throwing. His eyes were half-closed, peering malevolently at the other man. But Hamden was biding his time. His blue check shirt, made of much finer stuff than Bancroft's was torn open wide at the neck. In the centre of the long V of flesh was a fiery bruise where one of Bancroft's sledge-hammer blows had connected. Hamden's sleeves were down and clipped at the wrists, but in the right one was a long jagged tear from the elbow up, and over the shoulder. Blood gleamed beneath, where Hamden's thick, muscular arm was scratched. His face was bruised and bloodied, his black hair falling in ringlets over his forehead. The handsome foreman was no longer handsome. But he was far from finished. Both men had more than their share of pure, spirited guts.

The short wait was ended and the crowd's murmuring became a babble as, still crouching, Hamden began to move. Bancroft took two steps forward to meet him. The crowd roared.

Hamden led with his right. Bancroft blocked it. Hamden's left came round. A glancing blow to the temple. Bancroft swerved away. Shook his head as if stung. He came in again suddenly. His left crashed through Hamden's guard under the heart. Hamden gasped. He bent and clinched. Bancroft jabbed his shoulder. He spun away. Bancroft followed up, swung and missed. Hamden's come-back met him full face. Fresh blood spurted from his lips. He staggered. Hamden followed, throwing blows. Savagely, yet mechanically.

The crowd parted. The two fighters were travelling now towards the door. The arena had shifted a lot.

Bancroft went down in the narrow cleared space. Hamden fell over him, sprawled, spreadeagled. Bancroft was slow rising. But he was first up. He waited for Hamden. The foreman rose, turned. Bancroft hit him. Flush on the side of the jaw. He staggered, then righted himself mirac-

94

ulously. Bancroft swung again. He missed. But his next blow connected. Hamden's retaliatory one did, too. For a moment they stood slogging like robots, panting and grunting. Their fists like leaden weights. Their arms like pendulums.

Hamden staggered away and brushed up against the wall. To the right were the batwings, swinging gently. The fighters had crossed the room. The crowd had changed places with them.

Hamden moved mechanically as Bancroft charged. The lean man hit the wall. He turned. Hamden was by the window. Bancroft swung. He missed. His fist crashed through a pane. It came away dripping blood. Hamden rushed. His right drove into Bancroft's chest. The lean man fell and slid. He finished up before the batwings.

He rose, twisting. Hamden's fist grazed his cheek-bone. They stood apart. Then they leaned forward, swinging. Their bodies jerked tiredly. They gasped. The few blows thudded between gasps. Many of them missed entirely. Suddenly, Hamden launched an effective one.

Bancroft crashed against the left-hand door. His fingers caught the top. He held himself up. He swung away as Hamden rushed. They both swung on the door. Then let go. Back into the saloon. Both swinging and missing. Then focusing and hitting – wildly, desperately. Almost spinning over with their blows. Bancroft, a right to Hamden's head. Hamden staggering, flailing, hitting Bancroft on the side of the neck. Bancroft swinging again. Hamden spinning on his heels. Hamden backed against batwings now. Surging jerkily and missing. Bancroft staggering, head low, advancing. One mighty punch. His whole body behind it. Hitting Hamden square in the face.

The batwings parted to Hamden's body. He went clean through. They swung back against Bancroft's chest. He staggered. Then he lurched through them, too.

Hamden lay flat on the boardwalk, his head hanging in the dust. A piebald horse looked down meditatively into his face.

Hamden did not see the horse. His pouched, battered eyes were closed, his mouth open. Bancroft crossed the sidewalk slowly, swaying. He held the hitching-rail to steady himself as he looked down at his enemy. His chest heaving, he took in great gulps of the cool night air. He was fighting now to keep on his feet.

The first members of the crowd burst through the batwings. They did not seem to know the fight had finished until they saw the still form beneath the hitching-rail. Then one of them shouted: 'Hamden's finished!' The rest came out in a flood. Bancroft was butted by them as they gathered round the fallen ramrod. He kept tight hold on his leaning-post. Nobody took a great lot of notice of him. But he knew they would. He was in a very ticklish spot. Otson and the sheriff came out. Otson said: 'Good work, Gimpy. Let's get out of here.' But they could not get by. Right now the press was too thick. The sheriff said nothing. He was looking down at Hamden, and there was a queer smile on his face.

The young ramrod was coming round. Two men lifted him into a sitting position. His head lolled.

'Get him inside,' said somebody. They lifted him up.

Bancroft watched them dully, as they carried Hamden inside the Buckeye Bar. Then he saw Big Lou, who had regained consciousness just in time to see the last part of the fight. He had watched and listened. As usual, he meant trouble. His bull-like voice rose above all others as he bawled: 'There's the man you want. There's the man who killed Mike Calhoun—' The rest of his sentence was drowned in other cries as once more Bancroft became the cynosure of all eyes. There could be no mistake about who Lou meant, his thick pointing finger and glaring eyes bored at the lean man. But that was not all. Lou had not forgotten Perce Maddison, either. Nobody could lay him low and get away with it.

He waited for the din to subside a little, and then roared:

'We've got a fine sheriff. He ought to be strung up. He's hand in glove with this stranger—'

Bancroft, Maddison and Otson stood together by the hitching-rail. All eyes were turned to them now. Inside the saloon Hamden was coming round. He was forgotten. But his earlier words were not. He had said: 'Arrest that man.' Another voice echoed it now. And the crowd, like a single beast rather than separate individuals, growled menacingly.

Once more it was the unpredictable Maddison who acted first. He drew both his guns.

'Hold it!' he said.

The leaders of the crowd, Big Lou among them, halted in their tracks. Otson drew his guns. 'I'm right with yuh,' he said.

He had returned Bancroft's gun-belt to him and the lean man was buckling it on.

Loud enough for everyone to hear, Maddison said: 'You can hand that over again, Gimpy. I'm takin' you in.'

He stepped back suddenly. He was behind the lean

man. 'Don't try anythin', Gimpy,' he said. 'You, Pete – keep your eyes on the crowd.'

Almost imperceptibly, the sheriff covered his deputy, too. He said: 'I'm takin' this man in. He'll get a fair trial. If he's done all you say he has he'll pay for it. I'm still sheriff here. Right now I'm doin' my duty. That's what you elected me for—'

'We didn't elect yuh,' growled Big Lou.

Maddison disregarded this. He said: 'I'll shoot the first man who steps outa line – Gimpy, your guns.'

Slowly, Bancroft held then out. Maddison holstered one of his own, then took the gun-belt. Otson half-turned. 'Watch the crowd, Pete,' said the sheriff. His voice was almost threatening. Pete scowled, but did as he was told.

'Start walkin', Gimpy,' said Maddison.

Bancroft stepped off the sidewalk and began to limp along the dusty cart-rutted street. Maddison kept a few paces behind him, Bancroft's gun-belt slung over his shoulder, his own two guns out again and trained on his prisoner's back. The street before them was deserted. All life was behind them at the Buckeye Bar. As they made for the jail they might have been walking in a ghost town. Behind them deputy Otson began to back away from the crowd.

'It's what yuh wanted, ain't it?' he asked them. 'Personally, I think Bancroft's innocent. Stay right here an' think things over. I'll plug the first one who tries tuh follow. I shan't miss, 'cos I'm plenty mad.'

It took guts to walk away backwards while Big Lou and his cronies at the front watched him like wolves waiting to spring. Big Lou was the danger. Otson meant to plug him plumb centre if he moved.

So he backed cautiously, feeling his way among the cart-tracks, careful not to trip. The sheriff had certainly left him a fine job, blast him! What was his game, anyway? He knew Gimpy wasn't guilty – or did he?'

TEN

Big Lou did not move. But a pard of his, a villainous-looking younker called Gringo Jack, went for his gun. Otson fired coolly and deliberately. It was a long-range shot, but it found its mark. Jack dropped his gun and clawed at his chest, strangled curses spilling from his lips as he staggered to the edge of the boardwalk. He swayed there for a moment, then fell face forward into the roadway. Even as he toppled, Otson fired rapid shots over the heads of the crowd. Then he turned and began to run.

He heard Big Lou's bellow, answered by other shouts, and then a roaring babble that chilled his blood. A Colt crashed. Otson had a good start. He caught up with Maddison and Bancroft, who had turned to see what the fuss was about.

'I had to plug one of 'em,' panted Otson. 'The mob's wild. Git goin'.'

They were only a few yards from the office and jail. They sprinted the rest of the way. The mob almost filled the street, they came sluggishly as if they would engulf the three men.

Maddison unlocked the door and then went inside the

office. His gun still in his hand, Maddison turned to Bancroft.

'Back in the cell, Gimpy.'

'Are you crazy?' interposed Otson.

'It's the best way,' said Maddison.

Bancroft was out on his feet, but he looked at the sheriff with his old sardonic smile and took a step forward.

'Back up, Gimpy.' Maddison's voice was harsh. 'Get movin'. It's for your own good.'

Bancroft shrugged, then without another word allowed the sheriff to shepherd him to the cells.

The shutters had been built for defence. They were ironbound, with slits to see through and to take a rifle-barrel. Otson watched the street. If the mob wanted action, he was prepared to give it to them. He couldn't figure the sheriff. Gimpy shoud've been there with them with his shooting-iron instead of lying in a cell.

Maddison returned. He carried a scatter-gun. The mob's din became louder.

'Can yuh see 'em, Pete?'

'Not yet,' replied Otson. He turned. 'Perce, you can count me out on that hand you just dealt Gimpy. I'm on his side.'

'So am I,' said Maddison curtly. 'I guess I know what I'm doing—'

'They're here,' said Otson, looking through the shutters again.

Then they heard the bull-like voice of Big Lou roar: 'Fetch 'em out.'

Maddison stepped forward. He waited for a lull, then bawled: 'I've got a scatter-gun here, an' I'm quite prepared to use it if there's any funny business.' The last part of the sentence was almost drowned in the roar that greeted his voice.

The crowd had grown, but its nucleus remained in the forefront, Big Lou towering above all.

He shouted: 'We want Bancroft, an' we want that pesky deputy as well. He's killed Gringo Jack.'

Otson answered him. 'Jack asked for it.'

The crowd roared again. They were inflamed by liquor and by the fight they had seen; they were in a killing mood now, and they had a powerful leader in Big Lou. Otson wished now that he had plugged the big feller as well as Gringo Jack. The crowd probably would not have got this far then. But it would be fatal to shoot him now – the mob might rush. They were too near for the risk to be taken. The scatter-gun was the only thing if they did rush, although Otson hoped it would not have to be used. Some of the people in that crowd were decent fellows in ordinary times. They figured they had a grievance now. It would be tragic if some misguided waddy who figured he was just yelling for justice got hit as well as the leaders.

Otson did not know how Maddison felt about it. He looked formidable enough with the scatter-gun held ready at an aperture, and that grim, rather blank look on his handsome face. A queer cuss was Perce.

The crowd was still now. It hummed with argument and suggestion. Big Lou and his cronies were in a huddle. They were in the forefront. But they could not draw back now.

The crowd began to get restless again. Voices were raised in argument and threats. Someone threw a stone. It clattered on the shutters of the sheriff's office. But already some of those at the back had begun to drift back to the

Buckeye Bar. Big Lou's roar stopped them in their tracks.

'We'll settle for Bancroft. He's the snake we want. He's at the bottom of all the truoble in Elkanville. Turn him over, Sheriff, or we'll come in and take him.'

'I'm warnin' yuh, Lou,' shouted Maddison.

'Aw, quit,' bawled the big feller. 'You ain't got a chance. You won't get hurt if yuh let us have Bancroft pronto.' He took a few steps forward; the growling crowd surged behind hin. 'Root em out,' yelled somebody . . . . 'Yeh, rush 'em. . . .' 'Drag out the skunk—'

Maddison yelled hoarsely at the pitch of his lungs. 'I ain't warning yuh again.' Then, as the din subsided a little: 'This scatter-gun's liable to make a helluva mess out there.'

Big Lou and his cronies halted. They didn't like the sound of that scatter-gun. Maybe the sheriff wasn't bluffing after all. The people at the back kept on coming; they wouldn't get hit, anyway. The front ranks were thrust forward.

Otson watched the sheriff, awaited his cue. Maddison's lips drew back from his teeth; for a moment his handsome face was contorted. 'I'll show 'em,' he said.

He elevated the muzzle of thn scatter-gun and pressed the trigger. The gun boomed, the charge screamed just above the heads of the crowd. Otson grinned, took deliberate aim with his Colt, and let fly also. Big Lou's hat spun from his head.

'I've got another barrel left,' bawled Maddison. 'Next time I'll aim straight.'

The crowd was still. Slowly, his eyes shifting about him, Lou bent and retrieved his hat.

'You'll pay for this, Sheriff,' be shouted. But now he did not sound so truculent.

He turned. His cronies turned with him. The crowd fanned, milled around them, still arguing, still yelling threats, still keeping up their spirits with bravado. But they began to turn and shift. The gap between them and the jail became wider. Still shouting, they drifted back to the Buckeye Bar.

In his cell in the jail behind the sheriff's office Bancroft heard it all, but only vaguely understood it. He was aware that he was in danger. Well, he'd been in danger before – right now he was too tired to think about it. His brain was in a fog. He couldn't figure Perce Maddison lately, but he felt almost grateful to him for this cosy cell. He'd lain on plenty worse bunks than this one.

The din became less; he heard the shouting voices dull to a murmur, a murmur that lulled him. He did not find it hard to go to sleep. Come *mañana* maybe he'd be able to think better.

When he awoke the sun was streaming through the high, barred window. He groaned as he sat up; he was sore and stiff. But his brain was clear, and he felt devilish hungry. He rose slowly to his feet.

His limp was more pronounced as he crossed the cell to the iron-barred door. He listened. Behind him, outside, he could hear birds singing; not far away a horse whinnied. He could not near any human voices. And out front there, in the office, everything was silent as the grave.

'Hey!' yelled Bancroft. 'Maddison!' He shook the door till it rattled and rang, the sound echoing down the stone passage and among the other cells. Three others, Bancroft had noticed – all empty.

He listened again for a moment, then he yelled once more. This time his efforts bore fruit. There was a peevish

'All right, I'm coming,' from in front there.

'I want some grub,' yelled Bancroft. 'An' hurry it up, I'm mighty hungry.'

'All right,' said the muffled voice once more.

Satisfied, Bancroft returned to the bunk and sat down. He fumbled in the pocket of his tattered shirt and brought forth a rather battered little sack of 'makings'. He began to roll himself a quirly. Didn't do to worry about too many things at once. Right now he was hungry. He'd have a smoke. Then he'd have a meal. After that he could start to figure why he was here, and what he could do about it.

The voice had not sounded like the sheriff's or Otson's. It had sounded like that of an older man. Bancroft remembered seeing an old fellow around the jail sweeping and doing odd jobs. Anyway, whoever he was, he'd better hurry up or his prisoner was gonna be one hell of a nuisance.

But Bancroft need not have fretted; for, even is he lit up, the voice called: 'Hey, mister!'

'Yeh?'

'I'm getiin' yuh some grub. Ef'n you'll jest hold your peace for a few minutes.'

'All right, old-timer. But don't make it too long.'

The voice mumbled something distantly, and then there was silence. Dragging at his quirly, Bancroft rose and climbed on to the bunk. He looked through the barred window. The sight that met his gaze was not heartening but very common. It was not the first jail window Bancroft had looked out of on to the refuse-dumps and weed-plots. This area, which was unfenced, ran right on to the scrub and sparse grass that was the fringe of the range. Bancroft thought about the mob of last night, and wondered why none of them had come round back here. Probably because each single one of them felt safer as a unit of the mob rather than as an individual or member of a small group. That was the way with all mobs. Or, at least, most of 'em. Lucky for him, maybe.

As he stood there, Bancroft could see the range, rolling, gently undulating, right out to where the low hills squatted dimly in the morning mist. It wasn't so very late, then. He wondered where Maddison and Otson were. He jumped from the bench, and cursed as the jar sent pains shooting through his bruised limbs. He ran an exploring hand over his face. He was not a vain man, but right now he'd certainly like a peep at himself in a mirror.

His thoughts turned to the man who was the cause of his aches and pains. His thoughts were without rancour. Since last night, Kit Hamden had risen in his estimation. The young ramrod had proved he had guts and fighting ability. Bancroft had learnt fisticuffs in a tough hard school; he was a seasoned brawler, but the younker had given him a better run for his money than he had had for many a long day. And he had fought fairly. He had been scrupulously fair, with an inherent fairness that Bancroft realized must be ingrained in him. He had suspected Hamden of shooting Mike Calhoun and even of being the murderer of old Jeb Carter. In his hate of the young man's arrogance, he had been ready to believe him capable of any vileness. Now he wasn't so sure. Could a man who fought fairly, as Hamden had done, be a low-down dry-gulch merchant? You could never tell with people. Billy the Kid was reputed to be very tender with dumb animals. Did that signify? Bancroft's figuring was beginning to go haywire. He was glad when he heard footsteps in the passage.

A white-haired old man appeared at the door. He was a decrepit old cuss, bent and gnarled and rather grimy. He carried a tray on which was a plate of frizzled bacon and what looked like beans, a hunk of bread, and a steaming mug of dark-brown mud which was, presumably, coffee. However, from this collection rose quite an appetising odour. Bancroft started forward.

The old-timer stepped away from the door. 'Keep your distance, young feller,' he said. He grunted as he bent and placed the tray on the stone floor. He straightened up and drew a Colt .45 from the belt of his patched, dirty jeans.

He shook the gun in Bancroft's direction. 'Don't try anythin' funny,' he said. 'Or I'll shoot.'

The prisoner had no doubt he would. Judging by the way his palsied old hands were shaking, he might shoot anyway.

'I'll be good,' promised Bancroft. 'Would – would you mind lowering that gun jest a mite, old-timer?'

Obediently, the old man lowered it a little. Bancroft got ready to jump. He didn't want his toes shot off.

The old man began to push the tray along the floor with the toe of his foot. He removed the coffee from the tray, and continued to push it. He pushed it right underneath the cell door while Bancroft watched the wobbling gun with horrible fascination.

'Jest pick up thet tray, young feller,' said the old man. He waved the gun threatenily.

With commendable alacrity, Bancroft bent and picked up the tray. He turned and carried it across to the bunk.

'Now stay right where you are,' the old man told him. 'Don't turn round till I tell yuh.'

'All right,' said Bancroft. He heard the old cuss scrabbling around.

'All right. You kin turn round now.'

The cup of coffee was just inside the bars. 'So-long, son,' said the old-timer, and he disappeared.

'So-long, pop,' replied Bancroft rather weakly. He thought he heard a senile chuckle. Maybe it was just his imagination. The old guy had given him the jumps.

He had just finished his meal when he had another visitor. It was Doc Penders. The old jailer still had his gun in his hand as he let the medico into the cell and locked the door behind him.

'Yell when yuh want me, Doc,' he said.

'All right, Arizony,' replied Penders. He looked squarely at Bancroft, his dark young-old face expressionless.

'How yuh feeling, Gimpy?'

'All right.'

'All right? Yuh look kinda battered to me. I thought I'd come along an' fix yuh up.'

'Thanks, Doc. Seen Maddison?'

'Yeh.'

'What did he say?'

'Nothing much. Told me he put yuh in here after the fight, an' why. Personally, I don't think you're guilty, but I'm in the minority.'

'Thanks, anyway. What does Maddison think?'

'He didn't say. I guess he figures he's doin' his duty by the town.' By Penders' tone it was evident he did not think much of the sheriff, anyway.

'He must've gone out early this morning.'

'Yeh.'

'Is Otson there?'

'No, I haven't seen him. Only old Arizony.'

'Yeh, I've seen Arizony,' said Bancroft with a grim smile. 'The ol' coot don't seem very safe tuh me.'

'He ain't. Make no mistake about that,' said Penders. 'He'd shoot yuh as soon as bat an eyelash. He used to run with a wild bunch when he wuz younger. An' he ain't reformed either. He's jest getting too old to gallivant about. But he loves practising his marksmanship on prisoners. Let me see.' The doctor looked thoughtful. 'Old Arizony ain't shot a prisoner for about three months. He must be getting mighty impatient.'

Bancroft looked at the doctor. Penders' face was expressionless again.

He bent forward. 'Let's 'ave a look at you.' He placed his little black bag on the bunk.

Bancroft suffered himself to be prodded and probed.

'Apart from a few cuts an' bruises you're in pretty good shape,' said Penders at length. 'If you'll wash your face I'll fix it up for yuh. You certainly seem to've run it into everything handy since you got here. This is twice. Good job you can stand it.'

Bancroft smiled. 'I could do with a wash,' he said. He went to the door and yelled for Arizony.

He ordered the old man to get soap and water, a towel and a mirror. Ten minutes later he was gazing at the reflection of a face which, for the second time since he hit Elkanville, was adorned comically with sticking-plaster.

'You'll do,' said Penders. 'One good thing about bein' in jail, you will have to rest.' He yelled for Arizony.

'Don't worry, Gimpy,' he said. 'We'll figure something.'

He left the lean man to ponder over this last cryptic remark.

The day passed slowly for Bancroft. He sat and thought and smoked. Complete with Colt, old Arizony brought him his dinner. Again Bancroft asked for the sheriff. He had not returned.

However, half-an-hour later when the old man returned to take away the crockery, he said:

'Sheriff's here now, young fellar.'

'Is he? Tell him I want him then. Pronto!'

Another ten minutes passed, and Bancroft was on the point of yelling when boot-heels clattered heavily in the passage, and Maddison appeared at the doorway. He spoke hurriedly.

'I'm doin' all I can, Gimpy. All for the best. You gotta trust me.'

'I ain't so sure what you're doin' is for the best,' said Bancroft. 'Best thing you can do is let me out of here.'

'I can't do that now, Gimpy.'

'You dealt the hand all wrong, Perce,' said Bancroft grimly. 'An' I ain't forgettin'.'

'I'm sheriff here, Gimpy—'

'Yeh, so yuh keep sayin'—'

'An' I gotta be careful. I done what I thought was right last night, an' now I gotta play it through.'

'An' your playin' it through might mean a rope for my neck.'

'No, Gimpy. You're safer here than anywhere. In town your life wouldn't be worth a plugged nickel. An' if you left town now you'd be a hunted man. I've been talkin' with Judge Gorter. He ain't gonna call a trial for a bit. I'm sorta holdin' you on suspicion. Things'll blow over.

110

Thinkin' you're a dead pigeon, the killer of Mike Calhoun is liable to get careless an' give himself away. I'm workin' on an angle.'

'Wal, you can't pin this one on Shorty Matthews anyway. Everybody else wants to pin it on me so you might is well act on it.'

'Look, Gimpy, I—'

'You're playin' it safe, Perce,' said Bancroft. 'Safe for yourself.'

'I wish you'd trust me, Gimpy.'

'All right, maybe I will. I ain't got much choice, have I?'

'You won't regret it. With your help I'll bust this rotten town wide open.'

Bancroft did not speak again.

'So-long,' said Maddison, and he went.

When twilight came he had not returned. Bancroft did not see Otson at all. Maybe the deputy was cooking something up. Or he had been run out of town. The lean man wished he had controlled his temper enough to ask Maddison. Maybe Maddison was playing it right after all, although he was pretty high-handed. Bancroft did not know; he had nothing to go on. He merely had to leave things to his old pard and hope for the best.

The day had seemed ages long, but night was here at last. Bancroft paced up and down his cell like a caged beast and smoked till his eyes smarted and his head spun. The night was very dark and close, the high window of the cell, a faint square, ruled by half-a-dozen grim black stripes.

Bancroft had been locked up before, but he had never felt quite so impatient. He was in a killing mood. All his life he had been a trouble-shooter; it was not his way to

111

leave his fighting to other men. He had been suspected of two murders – in fact, it seemed they were being pinned on him. And without any real evidence – even circumstantial evidence. He wasn't getting a chance to do anything about it because the high-falutin', yaller-haired sheriff-boy who professed to be his pard, figured he could do it better. For a moment a gust of rage against Maddison seized him; then he sobered. Maybe he was misjudging the feller. Maybe Perce had it all figured out. His rage ought to be directed at the real killer, or killers of old jeb Carter and of Mike Calhoun. Still, the fact remained that Perce had no rights to act like he did last night. And if Bancroft had been in a fit condition then he might have shot it out with him. And then be torn to pieces by the mob. Yeh, that would've been fine and dandy. No, he guessed Perce had been right after all. So Bancroft's mind roamed in circles as the night marched on.

He heard old Arizony shuffling about out front and yelled for him.

The old man appeared, his Colt in his skinny fist, a scowl on his fare.

'You're a blamed nuisance,' he said. 'What d'yuh want now?'

'Ain't Maddison come back?'

'Nope.'

'You bin out, ain't yuh?'

'Yep.'

'Did yuh see Maddison?'

'Nope.'

'Do yuh know where he's gone?'

Tired of wasting words the old man shook his head this time.

'Have yuh seen Otson?'

Another shake of his dirty-grey head.

'Do yuh know where he's gone then?'

Arizony pursed his lips and waggled the gun, shaking his head once more.

'Argumentative old cuss, ain't yuh,' said Bancroft cynically.

'I don't want any lip from you, yuh young monkey,' said Arizony. He came a step nearer, wagging the Colt threateningly.

'Keep your distance, Pop. I might bite yuh.'

The old man snorted and, turning on his heels, stamped indignantly off down the passage.

So Maddison had not returned! As Bancroft listened to Arizony's retreating footsteps the first seed of suspicion was planted in his mind. A seed that multiplied slowly as he thought. A seed that later was to grow rapidly until it festered like an old saddle-sore.

As it proved, he was to have further terrible cause for suspicion that night.

Another hour or more passed. Bancroft realized it was getting late. From down the street came the raucous singing of drunkards, broken now and then by the tinkle of a piano, the shriek of a woman – sounds very common to cow-towns. Sounds very common to Bancroft's ears. He read them aright. It was getting close to turning-out time at the Buckeye Bar.

Gradually he became aware in his inner mind that the singing had changed to shouting. The harridan's shrieks became clearer. There were people in the street now and, listening close, he could not hear the piano any more. The voices became louder.

In the office, old Arizony heard them, too. He shuffled to the door, opened it and looked out. He shut the door and bolted it. The shutters were already drawn. He drew his Colt and placed it on the desk. Then he went into the passage to the armoury cupboard and selected a sawed-off shotgun. He always had been partial to shotguns. He was chuckling shrilly as he carried it back into the office. The prisoner called him, but he took no notice.

The din was louder now, ominously near. Stones rattled on the shutters. There were so many shouted threats and suggestions it was difficult to distinguish the complete words of any one of them. Arizony opened the shutter a little. A thin shaft of light traversed the board-walk and speared into the crowd. They roared. More stones came.

The general hubbub subsided a little and the voice of Big Lou boomed: 'Are yuh there, Sheriff?'

Arizony's voice was reedy with age, but it still had some carrying power. He shouted: ' No, the sheriff ain't here. But I am. An' I got a shotgun. An' I mean to use it.'

The crowd recognized his voice and a roar of laughter went up. The stones came thick and fast. Arizony felt like firing into the middle of them. When he was a younker he would've done. But with age he had learnt discretion. His spasm of rage had passed, and he felt old and trembly. And he could not think.

He essayed another peep through the shutters but, as the thin sliver of light streaked across the blackness, the shouting and laughter became intensified. But, in the brief glimpse, Arizony saw that many among the crowd had lit torches and held them aloft. The scene was awe-inspiring, the laughter had no mirth in it. It was brutal and savage. A rock hit the door with a thud that seemed to shake the building.

The crowd became quieter. The old man could hear Big Lou talking. Then he heard the prisoner yelling. He hesitated, looking at the door, then back in the direction of the cells.

'Let me out,' Bancroft was yelling, and calling Arizony by everything but his own name. Most of the names he called him were vile and outlandish. They would have been humorous had not the situation been so terrible.

Arizony cast another look at the door, cursed shrilly and, with the shotgun still in his hands, shambled into the passage. Bancroft was standing at the door of the cell. Despite the invective that had been spilling from his lips, he did not look mad. Just impatient.

He even smiled sardonically when he saw the old man. 'Let me out of here an' give me a gun,' he said.

'It's agin my orders, young feller, to—'

'What do orders matter now, yuh crazy ol' fool. D'yuh want that mob tuh tear yuh into little pieces? Let me out, gimme a gun' we'll keep 'em off. Quick – can't yuh hear them? C'mon, out with those keys, pronto.'

Arizony was moved by the urgency of the man's tones. For a moment he was panicky, he fumbled with the keys at his belt.

As he unlocked the cell-door the crowd was strangely quiet. Bancroft came out of the cell quickly. 'Guns,' he said.

Arizony led him to the armoury cupboard, and even as Bancroft sorted out his own guns, the old man was making for the office. As he reached it the outer door sagged as the battering ram hit it with a force that shook the building. Arizony halted, his expression and bearing no longer vacillating.

'First man who comes in gets it,' he shouted. As he spoke the ram hit the door again, tearing it from its hinges. It fell, just missing the desk. Men sprawled in with the battering-ram, a huge bulk of timber. Arizony snarled like an old wolf and pressed the trigger of the shotgun, even as Bancroft appeared behind him. The voice of Big Lou egged them on from the back, but it was his luckless tools, the wielders of the ram, who paid the price of his bravado. Two of them went down before the old man's flaming gun as he went down on his knees behind the desk.

The battering ram was dropped, guns raised, spitting in retaliation. Bancroft went down on one knee, firing through a swirling haze of smoke. A slug batted the Colt from his left hand, sending tingling pain to his elbow. He went flat on his stomach, fanning the hammer of his remaining weapon, spraying the doorway with withering, murderous fire.

Many of the luckless wielders of the ram went down in that first terrible blast from Bancroft and the old man. Others tumbled over them and so escaped their fate. His gun empty, Bancroft reversed it. He charged, lashing about him. But he did not stand a chance. Countless hands grasped him and lifted him, still struggling and fighting, from his feet.

Fists struck him from all sides. He was stunned, blinded, dazed with pain. The voice of Big Lou bawled: 'Don't rough him up too much, boys. Save him for the rope!' But in their blood-lusting frenzy many paid no heed to their leader. The blows continued to fall until the victim of their savagery ceased to feel them any more.

Behind the desk old Arizony lay in a pool of blood, the top of his head blown off by a slug from a Colt fired at close range. He who had fought the law so many times in his long life had finally died fighting for it. In those last swift glorious moments he had re-lived the smoke-ridden, bloody legends of his youth and, at their climax, he died as he had lived. For whom or for what he was fighting at that moment did not matter much anyway.

ELEVEN

Bancroft came to his senses to find himself in the saddle, his hands tied behind him, the centre of a yelling mob, fearsome in the wavering light of torches. At one side of him, also on horseback, was Big Lou; and, on the other side of him, one of Lou's cronies who was known as Long Jack. The prisoner was still badly dazed; to him the whole scene had the strange fluctuating quality of a dream. At first he had thought Big Lou and Long Jack, strange characters both of them, were steering him through rushing seas; then again, he thought he was being borne along by a stampeding herd of cattle. He felt the remote terror of a nightmare; he was sweating and his vision was obscured by a red mist. Only later did he realize that the red mist was blood running into his eyes from a gash in his temple. Even when he became fully aware of his peril, of the terror that was real, he could not see anything clearly. There seemed to be hundreds of people, all yelling and screaming for his blood. A sluggish, bobbing mass illumined garishly by the light of dozens of flickering, waving torches.

Maybe there were a hundred people all told, probably less; and probably half a dozen torches at most. The lynch-

118

mob was composed mainly of the very worst elements of Elkanville. Bancroft knew that many others who had yelled and threatened as loud as the rest would have slunk away by now, or were hovering timorously on the outskirts. And the more law-abiding people had shut their doors and windows tight, and, with averted eyes, their ears and their consciences, too. Sardonically, Bancroft weighed things up and figured he hadn't got a Chinaman's chance – whatever that was, it wasn't much. He had seen lynch-mobs before – he knew their ways. Once they had their victim and had started with him they didn't stop till they'd finished with him. Then they went and got roaring drunk. In the morning, those of them who weren't wholly black-hearted maybe got to thinking whether they had done the right thing or not. By then it was too late to do anything about it anyway. And a week later they were bragging about the way they had strung that coyote up!

It was no dream now, no terror-ridden nightmare. Bancroft was fully awake. But he still felt kind of sleepy and he wasn't scared any more. He'd never figured he'd live to a ripe old age; maybe he'd meet somebody who was too good for him and go out swiftly in a haze of smoke, the scent of burnt powder in his nostrils. But he never figured he'd finish like this, at the end of a lynch-mob's hemp. He guessed he'd been kinda let down by a friend. He wondered what had happened to Perce. Maybe it wasn't his fault after all.

The mob had reached the end of Main Street. There was not so much yelling now – more individual purpose or at least the illusion of such; each man buoyed up by the thought that he was administering rough justice. That was the way to treat a murdering coyote – be a lesson to others like him. It didn't need thinking about much, really; each man let himself be carried along by his neighbours. And everybody looked at the leader, Big Lou. They were not disappointed, the slowthinking big fellow was very aware of his new-found importance. He had been a mere tool for quicker-witted men; maybe he now envisioned himself boss of the town. The fact remained that at this moment he was a leader, and he meant to carry things through with a flourish.

'Let's have him agin the cottonwoods,' he yelled. Then he turned to Bancroft and said: 'Look alive, yuh coyote, 'cos you won't be able to fer long. We're gonna string you up higher'n a kite.' Those around him laughed and encouraged. Lou raised his voice again and shouted: 'We'll show people they can't monkey with the townsfolk o' Elkanville.'

A roar greeted these words; no great orator could have received a better ovation. There were cries of 'You bet!' 'Teach 'em a lesson,' and as the cavalcade halted on the edge of the small grove of cottonwoods many began to call for 'The rope – the rope—!'

Big Lou steered Bancroft's mount under the largest of the cottonwoods, until his head was directly beneath a long, smooth bough. Long Jack produced the rope and deftly made a noose. The crowd was silent except for a faint shuffling and humming. This rose to a concerted gasp of triumph, of savagery, as Long Jack slung the rope across the bough. The noose swung over with a hiss only perceptible to Bancroft and two or three others. The noose hit the lean man in the face.

Big Lou guffawed: 'It knows its mark!' he said.

As Bancroft sat there, with the noose swinging gently a

120

few inches from his eyes, his face – though bloody – was still decorated by the plaster which Doc Peuders had used.

Big Lou said: 'You ain't pretty enough to be hanged. We can't see your pretty face well enough.'

He reached forward with one huge hand, caught hold of the corner of a strip of plaster, and tore it savagely from Bancroft's cheek. The lean man jerked forward in the saddle. Fresh blood ran from the newly opened wound. Big Lou reached out again. His nails scrabbled at Bancroft's other cheek, where a long strip of plaster ran under his chin. Big Lou caught hold and tugged again. Bancroft almost fell from the saddle. Long Jack held him. Bancroft looked at Lou and cursed him, his eyes alight with murder. The big man laughed in his face.

'Get on with it,' yelled somebody. 'Yeh, string him up.' 'Quit playin' around!' 'H'ist him!'

Long Jack reached up to put the noose around Bancroft's neck. But his attention, like that of all those around him, was suddenly diverted. Once again, the looped rope buffeted Bancroft's face. But to him now it was a mere love-tap.

There was the sound of drumming hoofs out on the range coming nearer, coming fast. Men forgot Bancroft; and, turning, fingered their guns or looked around for an opening, a chance to slip away and watch developments in safety.

'What's the matter with yuh?' bawled Lou. 'What's that? Who's comin'?'

Nobody could answer him yet, but necks were craned, eyes strained to pierce the darkness, until the shapes of the oncoming equipage, horses and horsemen loomed from the depths of it.

The carriage drew to a halt, the horsemen drew abreast each side of it. A long line of them. A torchlight illuminated the craggy features and white hair of Burt Burgoyne, and the beautiful smooth face, dark eyes and shimmering dark hair of his daughter Miriam. In the saddle, above the others, the noose still dangling in his face, Bancroft saw it all through a faint reddish haze. He was surprised to see Miriam in her usual place beside her father. He was more surprised to see that astride his horse beside the carriage, at Miriam's side, was Kit Hamden, a bit beplastered and the worse for wear, but steady and purposeful-looking. Doc Penders was there, too. And Tiger Macintosh, and Three-ton Thurston and his tow-headed assistant, Pinky. And others – probably Burgoyne men – who were armed with shotguns. There was no sign of the sheriff or his deputy.

The crowd was hushed now. Big Lou looked around him, seeking an outlet. Behind Bancroft there was only a small cluster of men. Lou turned his horse.

Then he froze in the saddle as the decisive tones of Hamden rang out: 'Stay put, Lou, or you're liable to get plugged.'

Long Jack, who had made an imperceptible movement to follow his pard, tried to look as if he was not there any more. Old Man Burgoyne stood up from his seat in the buggy. His voice quavered a little but was resonant as he said: 'As long as I'm here to stop it, there'll be no lynch-law in Elkanville.'

He sat down. He had said all he wanted to say to the rabble. But they were quelled. Mayhap it pleased his old heart to think that they were quelled by his voice rather than by the guns of his minions.

He frowned slightly as Three-ton Thurston said: 'Anybody daid?' and another man laughed. The old man spoke to his daughter. She in her turn spoke to Kit Hamden.

The young ramrod kneed his horse forward. 'Open up!' he said imperiously.

The crowd parted sluggishly to let him through. He rode up to the group under the big cottonwood. Both Big Lou and Long Jack drew back as far as they could, leaving Bancroft alone, erect on the horse, tattered and bleeding, his hands tied behind him, the hanging noose swinging gently before his face.

'Can yuh swing him round, Gimpy?' said Hamden gruffly.

Bancroft was surprised at his erstwhile opponent's use of his nickname. With a gentle pressure of his knees, he guided the horse around until he had his back to Hamden. Now he was facing out to the quiet west of the range, only a small knot of silent men between him and the freedom of the windblown grassy spaces. Behind him, the mob and his deliverers and – touching him now – his erstwhile enemy, who was sawing away with a knife at the bonds on his wrists. Then, as the threads began to part, Hamden began to speak softly. He said.

'As soon as you're free, get goin'. My men won't shoot at you, for fear o' hitting somebody else. The mob's in their way, most of 'em on foot. You'll get a good start. D'yuh hear me?'

Slowly, Bancroft nodded his head. He did not speak. His brain was racing. It seemed too good to be true. Was it true? Was it genuine? Was his enemy giving him this chance, or was it just a trick? Was he to be shot down like a rabbit instead of having his neck stretched like a turkey? But surely they wouldn't stop the hanging just to do it another way? The ropes parted and he received a sharp nudge in the back. He kicked his heels savagely into the horse's flanks and the beast started forward.

He was out in the open, the wind whipping at his face. Somebody shouted. He heard two shots but did not feel or hear anything near him.

The horse was all out now in a triumphant gallop. He seemed as glad to get away from the mob as Bancroft was. He was a long, rangy, powerful beast. Bancroft wondered where they had got him from. Whoever his owner was, he was probably lamenting his loss right now. Fancy picking a grand beast like this for a lynch-nag. Bancroft grinned derisively. *Amateur necktie party!* He could afford to grin now! But if he wished to continue grinning, he had to keep on riding.

He wiped his tattered sleeve across his eyes. The blood had dried; he could see better now. Here and there above him in the dark sky a few stars winked. Their presence was heartening, their light enough to ride by. Bancroft was thankful there was no moon. All around him was grassland, knee-high to the horse in places. The wind whipped through his hair.

He had no hat, no gun, no food, no water. But right now, he was free. He had been resigned to a certain and ignominious death. It was glorious to be free. The cool wind cleared his scattered senses, the power and speed of the beast beneath him seemed to give him strength. The beast was eating up distance with a long, loping gallop. He seemed tireless. And although they had been travelling quite a time now, the rider had not yet heard sounds of pursuit. Lucky for Bancroft that the 'amateur necktie party' had selected such a mount for its prospective offering to the evil sport of old Judge Lynch.

The iron-shod hoofs beat a steady tattoo on the sod, the grass parted and swish-swished against the horse's legs. And suddenly, like an echo of this tattoo and rhythm, Bancroft thought he heard other hoofs heating in the distance. He reined in the horse, giving him a breather, and listened.

Yes, he was being chased sure enough. But there didn't seem to be many of them. It almost sounded like one horse! Bancroft waited a little longer. He had confidence that his own mount would be able to forge ahead once more.

As the sound of galloping hoofs became clearer, Bancroft was certain there was only one rider. Bancroft was unarmed. Must he turn and run? He decided to take a chance. A few moments later he was glad he had done so, for a familiar voice yelled. 'Gimpy!'

'Here,' he replied.

A horse hove in view, atop it the tall, thin figure of Pete Otson.

The deputy drew rein beside Bancroft. 'I'm ridin' with you, Gimpy,' he said.

'There's no need to, Pete,' Bancroft told him. 'Still, I'm glad tuh see yuh all in one piece. I wondered what happened to yuh.'

'Big Lou an' his mob ran me outa town before they came after you. I slipped along the backs an' rustled out Doc Penders an' Three-ton an' Tiger an' one or two more. They rode to the Burgoyne ranch. They figured whatever

ol' Burt thought about you he wouldn't tolerate a lynch-
ing. They were right. I figured I'd best keep outa sight.
Maybe I could help yuh get away better that way. Hamden
beat me to it.'

'Deliberately, too,' said Bancroft. 'I wuz surprised.'

'I ain't surprised at Hamden any more. I guess I like the
guy a bit better now. Whatever else he might be, he *is* a
square-shooter. I guess we wuz barking up the wrong
gumtree, Gimpy.'

And as they passed over the border into Mexico, Otson
illustrated this last cryptic remark.

'Maddison lit out early this morning. When I asked him
if he needed my help, he was quite ornery about it. I told
him that if he was workin' on somethin' that'd clear you I
wanted to be in on it. I felt like sluggin' the big skunk. He
went out in a tantrum. I gave him a start, then followed.
He went through the foothills, making for the border, but
further along the line than here. I lost him.

'I went back to Elkanville. Big Lou tried to pick a fight
with me, but I wriggled out of it. He'd got too many
backin' him, an' I wanted tuh keep all in one piece. I
heard Perce had come back later in the day, but I didn't
see him.'

'I saw him then,' said Bancroft.

'Well, I didn't see him again till late tonight – I saw him
ride in. He looked like he'd been ridin' hard. He didn't
see me. I expected him to go to the oflice, but he didn't.
He went to, of all places, the Buckeye Bar. I didn't mean
to go in after him an' show myself, so I snuck along that
alley at the side an' peeped through the window. I had the
shock o' my life then. Maddison was over in a corner at the
end of the bar. An' he was talking to Big Lou an' that pard

o' his, Long Jack – I might tell yuh, Gimpy, Perce'd bin acting kinda funny for quite a time, but I figured it was because that Burgoyne filly was dandlin' him around. Now I figure it might be somethin' a damn sight worse than that. I was mighty suspicious. Him an' Lou wasn't arguin' – they seemed to be havin' a mighty friendly an' interesting conversation. Long Jack left 'em an' I lost sight of him. Lou an' the sheriff had got their heads together like long-lost brothers.

'The sheriff leaves the place an' I dodges round front to watch him, an' he rides outa town. For a bit I didn't know whether to follow him or not. Then I figures I might be doin' better by hangin' around there an' awaiting developments. So I dodges down the alley to the window again. I can't see Big Lou anywhere now. Or Long Jack. I found out where Long Jack was sooner than I expected. He came up behind me in the alley an' slugged me. Lou must've sent him out to reconnoitre before the sheriff went, an' he spotted me spying.

'When I came to I wuz in the Buckeye Bar an' Big Lou was proposing that I be run outa town. That I was spyin' an' meddlin' an' interfering with the law I was supposed to stand up for. Everybody thought it was a great laugh – I guess they wanted a little somethin' to get 'em in the mood for the big show o' the night, in which you was to be the star performer. They wuz quite gentle with me really. Anyway, I wuz plenty fit enough to slink back along the back and rustle up the boys. The rest yuh know, Gimpy.' The drone of Otson's voice ceased. He threw out his hands, then brought them down with a final smack on his thighs.

For a moment there was silence except for the rhythmic

thud of the horses' hoofs, the swishing of the grass, the soughing of the night wind. Then Bancroft said:

'So you figure Maddison sorta tossed me tuh the wolves, hey?'

'What else?'

'Yeh, it suttinly looks that way,' said Bancroft. 'To tell the truth, I had the same kind of suspicions myself jest after Maddison pulled me in. He wuz so strange about it all. But I couldn't figure why. Why, Pete?'

'I can't figure why, either, Gimpy.' Then, with a touch of his old dry humour: 'Unless the poor galoot's gone completely crazy after all.'

'I'm beginning to get an idea at somethin' maybe a durn sight worse than that,' said Bancroft grimly. 'An' a durn sight less innocent—'

Otson grunted, then said slowly:

'I thought maybe as Maddison had suddenly gotten to hate Calhoun so much, he might've plugged him. It could've been him just as easily as anybody else yuh might know, Gimpy.'

'Yeh. But it might even go deeper than that. Our tame sheriff's turned out tuh be a load o' dynamite, Pete, unless I miss my guess.' Bancroft's voice was becoming slow and husky. The terrific beating he had taken was beginning to tell on him at last. He felt sapped of all energy and deadly tired. He said finally, slowly, as if he could not puzzle his brains over it any longer that night: 'Whatever lies at the bottom of all this, Pete, I mean tuh find out.'

'I'm right with yuh there, Gimpy.'

TWELVE

'I know an ol' man,' said Otson. Then he paused. Bancroft was slumped in the saddle, his head on his breast. He seemed to be asleep. But he was not.

He said: 'You were sayin', Pete?' His voice was weary.

'I know an old Mexican who'll give us shelter an' fix you up proper, Gimpy. It's along here someplace. I hope I can find it in the dark. I think if we strike off the trail about here. . .' Otson led the way.

Bancroft guided his own mount after him with a gentle, mechanical pressure of his knees. They drew abreast of the ex-deputy and his rawboned bay gelding. The grass-land was clotted with outcroppings of rock, patches of shrub and here and there a tree. This was a dry, arid land; even now, at night, the air was oppressive. The long, dry brittle grass swished and crackled against the horses' legs. They travelled at a steady, jogging pace now, the hoofbeats muffled by the grass, the sound seeming to come like an echo from the depths of the dry earth beneath.

This rhythmic pulse sounding beneath him, beneath the smooth see-sawing of the horse's back, lulled Bancroft so that he did not want to talk any more, or think any more, but just sink into a drowsy coma. His legs were bowed tightly around the horse's body, his feet firm in the stirrups. He let the muscles of his body relax. He slumped, letting his head drop like a dead weight on his chest once more. This relaxation soothed the swelling, throbbing ache that seemed to encompass the whole of him.

Many years ago he had learnt the usefulness and beauty of this half-sleep in the saddle. He was thankful that Pete did not seem inclined to talk any more.

A faint dust rose from the grass disturbed by the horses. It surrounded Bancroft like a faint, smoky haze. He looked sideways; to him now, Pete and his horse were only an indistinct silent organism, just a moving shape. Bancroft closed his eyes, let his head nod gently with the jogging of the saddle. His arms hung lax, the reins loose in his hands. He left everything to the horse. The reliable beast kept steadily with its companion.

How long he rode in a half-dream Bancroft did not know. He became suddenly alert as they hit rocky, uneven ground, and the horse's gait became less steady.

'D'yuh know where we are, Pete?' he said.

For a moment Pete did not reply. He, too, had been dozing. Finally he drawled: 'Yeh, I think so. We ain't got very far tuh go now unless I'm very much mistaken.' He blew out a distressful gust of breath. 'Gosh, ain't it hot. An' so durned dark, too.'

Bancroft's horse slithered on loose shale as they descended a slight declivity. They reached the bottom. The horse snorted, picking disgustedly at the ground with his front feet.

'Take it easy, old-timer,' said Bancroft. 'I don't like this pesky country no more'n you do.'

'I figure we got about another coupla miles to go, then we'll hit more grassland an' a narrow trail,' said

Otson. 'The trail leads to a little settlement. It ain't got a name. Its people scratch a bare livin' from the soil thereabouts. Ol' Guido keeps a little store in the outskirts. In his spare time he's a bandit. Bein' a lawman I ain't supposed tuh know him. But he's an old friend o' my father's. The old man had some queer an' some very good friends. Guido was both. I guess now I ain't a lawman any more, it don't matter whether I know Guido or pretend not to. I guess he's a nice kind o' bandit anyway – the ol' skunk.'

Otson delivered himself of this startling narrative in his usual drawling, laconic tones. Bancroft could not think of any rejoinder so he kept his mouth shut. In Mexico, banditry seemed to be the spare-time hobby of every male over twelve years of age. He was looking forward to meeting old Guido.

They jogged on in silence for a time, lulled into a stupor by the humid air and the motion of the horses. Then Bancroft said suddenly:

'Did Perce Maddison know of your association with this ol' bandit?'

'Nope. Perce an' me called there once when we were over here seekin' information. We had drinks an' chow. Guido and me pretended we'd never seen each other afore. Him bein' a peace officer, Perce mightn't have liked me bein' associated with a bandit.'

'Did Perce know Guido was a bandit?'

'Maybe. Anyway, Guido's got quite a rep if not as a bandit as a man who'll take in anybody who's on the run.'

'Like us.'

'Yeh, like us.'

The first heavy drops of rain fell, plummeting from the

sky like pebbles until they splashed into a thousand crystals on their shoulders.

'Here it comes,' said Otson.

The rain fell faster.

'Wal, at least it'll cool us down a bit,' said Otson.

He raised his voice at the end of his sentence but Bancroft did not hear him. The rain came down suddenly in a blinding sheet, thunderous, cutting off every sound but its own, cutting all vision.

'Keep close, Pete,' Bancroft bawled. But he did not know whether the ex-deputy had heard him or not.

In a moment he was soaked to the skin. The cool water was a balm to his bruised and lacerated body. It beat on his unprotected head, ran down his face in rivulets, making his wounds smart. He licked his lips, sucked the sweet moisture into his parched mouth. It was good.

After a half-hour of solid pounding violence the rain abated as quickly as it began. The air was cooler, fragrant with the scent of wet grass as the horses left the hard ground and plunged into rangeland once more. But it was lonely rangeland. In all their long ride the two men had not seen or heard a living soul in the night, not even a straying steer.

About ten minutes later they hit the trail. They turned their horses' heads and set them at a canter.

A small cluster of lights proclaimed the little settlement they were seeking. They reined in outside a long single-storey log cabin on its outskirts.

The shutters were up at the two long windows, one at each side of the door. Here and there a chink of light showed. Otson rapped three times sharply on one of the shutters. They waited a moment. They heard no sound from inside but suddenly the door beside them opened a little.

'Who's there?' said a gruff voice.

The ex-deputy slid from his horse. 'It's me, Guido – Pete Otson.'

The door opened wider, and the form of a little tubby man was silhouetted there. The light that streamed out gleamed on the barrel of the sawn-off shotgun he held in his hands.

'I recognize your voice, Pete,' he said. 'Come in.'

'I've brought a friend with me, Guido,' said Otson quickly. 'A good friend.'

'Bring him in, too.'

'We'll bed our horses first.'

'The stable is open, Pete. There is fresh straw. Behind the door there is a bag of oats and a lantern.'

'Thanks, Guido.'

'Thank you,' said Bancroft.

He was strangely moved by the old Mexican's old-world courtesy. He was one of the old school and was no doubt a courteous bandit who stole only from the rich and respected the honour of beautiful ladies. His speech, too, was excellent, with only the faintest sign of a Mexican accent.

After they had seen to their horses they returned to the cabin. A thin sliver of light cut into the blackness from the door that was still ajar. Otson pushed it open, and they went inside.

The place in which they found themselves had all the appearance of a Western general-store, which sold anything from riding gear to chewing-tobacco and boot-laces. The little fat Mexican was standing in the aperture

133

at the end of the long counter. Behind him was another open door.

'Come through into the back,' he said.

He was very dark, podgy-faced, clean-shaven; the light shone on his head, which was completely bald except for a little fuzz over each ear. The two men followed him into the living-room, which was full of heavy furniture and profusely bestrewed with gay carpets, many of them hung, in the Spanish manner, from the walls.

Guido turned again, saying: 'Sit down, my friends—' Then he threw up his podgy hands in an extravagant gesture, his little dark eyes widened, his mouth forming an 'O'.

'You are drenched,' he said. Then he looked straight at Bancroft. 'And you, my friend, have been hurt badly.'

'This is Gimpy Bancroft, Guido,' said Otson laconically. 'You ain't seen him at his best, I fear. He *is* kinda mussed-up. I told him you wuz the greatest li'l medicine man this side o' the Rio Grande.'

Guido shrugged eloquently. 'Always the flatterer, Pete. However, I will do my best not to disappoint your friend.'

He did not. And when Bancroft who, patched up once more and clad only in his trousers, was seated before a man-sized meal, complimented him on his skill, he merely shrugged again and said: 'It ees nothing.'

Bancroft did not speak again for quite a while. He was too hungry. Otson was not in quite such a bad way so, while his pard was gorging himself on luscious steak, fried onions, potatoes and beans, washed down with hot sweet coffee, he regaled Guido with a chronicle of their adventures.

Then Guido dropped his bombshell. Unconsciously, he

gave the two men the first lead which was to help them to unravel the torturous, callous plot which was behind the Elkanville crimes.

He said: 'Your friend, the sheriff you mention, the one who came here with you that day, he has been here since. Last week I theenk—'

'What was *he* doin' over here last week?' Bancroft said.

Otson said: 'Was he alone?'

Guido replied: 'Yes.'

Otson said: 'What did he come for?'

'Just to buy things. A saddle blanket, some cigarettes, one or two more leetle things. An' I bought some gold-dust from him.' There was dead silence for a moment.

Then Bancroft cursed forcibly and said: 'You bought gold-dust from him?'

'Yes, I often buy gold-dust.'

'Did you ask him where he got it?'

Guido shrugged. 'I never ask questions. And, after all, ees he not a sheriff?'

'Was there a lot?'

'Four bags. Eet is currency in this part of Mexico, you know.'

'Yeh, I know,' said Bancroft bitterly. 'He probably sold a lot more at carefully selected places. I guess I can tell you where he got it from.'

'It can't be,' said Otson softly.

'Can't it?' said Bancroft. 'Don't you see, Pete, that it's the answer to everything?'

'Yeh, I do. But Perce Maddison—'

'I guess you an' me didn't know Perce Maddison as well we thought we did. I guess nobody knows him properly. An' maybe if he hadn't come here like he did *we* would

135

never have found him out.' Bancroft began to laugh softly and horribly. 'No wonder the sheriff wanted the good people of Elkanville to lynch the man they thought had killed ol' Uncle Jeb an' Mike Calhoun!'

'You'd better get to bed, Gimpy,' said Otson. 'You've taken quite a beating. You ain't made of iron even if you think you are.'

'All right,' said Bancroft. He laughed rather wildly again. 'But you're convinced, ain't yuh, Pete?'

'Yeh, I guess I am,' said Otson. 'Perce Maddison! I guess I'll never properly understand human nature. We'll talk about it in the morning, eh, Gimpy?'

Bancroft was more sober now. 'I guess it'd be best,' he said. 'I guess neither of us can think clearly tonight. Maybe I'm wrong, maybe there's an explanation.' They left it at that.

By the morning their heads were clearer. But their weighing of pros and cons in the case against Perce Maddison did not clear him. Rather it did seem to make the indictment against him more likely to stick. All they needed now was proof.

Although Guido said Bancroft was not really fit enough to travel, the lean man would not stay. And Otson did not add his own voice to the old man's persuasions. Guido shrugged. After breakfast they bade him *adios* and rode on their way. And, as they rode Bancroft told Otson what he meant to do.

They had dinner in a little cantina in a Mexican settlement of adobe huts while ragged peons dozed in siesta and mongrel curs snapped at flies. It was very hot again as they rode away after their short rest, their departure watched by dull, half-closed eyes, their faces streamed with sweat.

At twilight they crossed the border again into El Paso, in the corner of Texas. There they caught a train. The horses came along at the back in the van.

They sat at a window as the train chugged through the moonlit range of the Pecos.

'Great country this,' said Otson. 'I lived here when I was a kid.'

'So did I,' said Bancroft. 'An' I keep coming back to it.'

Time passed quickly as they reminisced. They were surprised when the conductor yelled out: 'Next stop, Stockton!'

'Here we are,' said Bancroft.

They knocked up a drowsy clerk in the hotel in main street. He booked them a room and directed them to the stables. When they returned from bedding the horses down he was fast asleep.

'Still the same ol' sleepy burg,' said Bancroft.

He took their key from the board behind the youth's head, and they crept upstairs.

When they woke it was raining. They had breakfast, then went outside. It was still raining, so they went to a nearby general store and bought a slicker apiece.

'We got a lot o' ridin' tuh do, Pete,' said Bancroft. 'An' we don't hafta keep gettin' wet.'

The rain was pelting now. They slung their slickers around their shoulders and, keeping to the sidewalk and in shelter as much as possible, they walked down the street. Bancroft led the way. He turned into the open door of a small redbrick building. There was a passage with a long bench against one wall. A big man sat on the end of the bench, cleaning a gun. He looked up as they entered, then started to his feet.

137

'Bancroft,' he boomed and held out his hand.

'Howdy, Matters,' said the lean man. They shook hands. 'The major in?'

'Yeh,' said Matters. 'Go right in.'

Bancroft turned to Otson. 'Would yuh mind waiting a bit, Pete?'

'Nope. Go ahead.'

'Tell him your Injun story, Matters,' said Bancroft.

The big man grinned. 'Sure thing.'

When Bancroft entered the office the little white-haired old man behind the desk rose to his feet and held out his hand. They shook.

'Glad to see you, Bancroft. Sit down.'

'Thank you, major.'

There was a faint smile on the old man's face, his keen blue eyes twinkled as he said: 'So you've come back, my lad?'

'Yes, Major, I've come back.'

'To join up with us again?'

'Yes.'

'I thought you would. You were never cut out to be a wet-nurse to sick dogies.' His face sobered. 'You've been in trouble, haven't you? Let's hear about it.'

Bancroft leaned across the desk.

Matters had finished his Injun story and Otson was chortling and slapping his thighs when Bancroft called him. Otson went into the office with him.

When the two men left the office they both wore little silver badges pinned to the underside of their vests – Bancroft that of a United States marshal and Otson that of a deputy marshal.

Later, as they rode to the station, Bancroft said: 'I guess

138

I ain't never gonna get tuh be a cowpoke, Pete. I wuz a marshal, an ornery trouble-shooter for eleven years. I resigned and thought I'd get me a peaceable job.' He snorted. 'But not me! I guess trouble jest naturally follers me around. Look what a mess o' trouble I brought to Elkanville.'

'You didn't bring it, Gimpy,' Otson told him.

Bancroft shrugged. 'Hum – anyway, here I am toting a badge again.'

The ranch buildings of Burgoyne's Curly W drowsed in the afternoon sun. Its rays bounced from the hard-baked soil. The buildings sprawled as if beaten down by the glare. The large, two-storey ranch house, which was painted white, was a shimmering dazzle. There was not a human being in sight. In the corral two old horses dozed. Beneath the meagre shade of a dying tree which overhung the long one-storey bunk-house lay an old black dog. His eyes were closed, his hoary muzzle rested on his forepaws.

Slowly he opened one bleary eye, his ears twitched. Then he raised his head slightly, turning it. Round the bend of the trail which led to the big gates, were coming a horse and a rider. The old dog watched them speculatively until they passed under the archway. Then he dropped his head on his paws and dozed once more. He had recognized them.

The rider dismounted at the corral and hitched his horse to the rails. He began to walk across the yard, a tall broad man with a handsome expressionless face and long blond hair waving from beneath his Stetson.

Another man came out of the ranch house. Their paths met. They looked at each other guardedly.

'Hallo, Hamden,' said the first man.

'Hallo, Sheriff,' was the reply. Then: 'Have yuh caught any murderers lately?'

No flicker of emotion crossed the other's face. 'No,' he said.

'Any sign of Bancroft?'

'No.'

'Or the man or men who dry-gulched Big Lou and Long Jack?'

'You know, I think Bancroft did that as well.'

'Yeh, I know. But I don't think he did. I don't see why he should.'

'He's the only one who would've.'

'It's convenient to think that, I guess,' drawled Hamden. 'But I don't see why he should come back just to put paid to Lou an' Jack.'

'Revenge. They nearly put paid to him.'

'You can't convince me.'

'I can't figure you, Hamden,' said the sheriff. 'You used to hate Bancroft until he gave you a beatin'. Now you seem to be on his side. It was you who gave him the chance to get away.'

'You can't prove that,' said Hamden. 'No,' he added reflectively, 'I guess you'll never understand me, Perce. No more than I'll understand you. You an' Bancroft were pards an' now you've turned right against him.'

'We wuz pards till I found him out.'

Hamden grinned tightly. 'Keep tryin', Perce,' he said. Deliberately he passed the sheriff. The latter turned and stood watching him for a moment. He was making for the stables. He did not look back.

Even as the sheriff continued on his way, Hamden came

out with his horse. He mounted and set off across the range. Maddison had his foot on the bottom step of the veranda when Miriam Burgoyne came out of the house.

'Hallo, Perce,' she said. 'Dad's in the back. Go in to him.'

'I want to see you first, Miriam,' he replied.

'What about?'

'I think maybe you can guess,' he said, softly. 'Don't play with me. Let's go somewhere where it's a bit more private.'

The girl shrugged. 'I hate mysteries, Perce,' she said. 'Come on back of the bunk-house.'

He said no more but followed her. His eyes were on her all the time. She walked gracefully in her embroidered high-heel riding boots. Her fringed leather skirt flared slightly as it swung. Her figure was shapely, tapering upwards from the waist to broad shoulders and a proud neck. She was hatless; the wealth of her hair, so often tucked under a slouch hat, now hung in shimmering waves. Maddison drew abreast with her, watching her beautiful, disdainful profile which so often maddened him, the brown column of her neck which disappeared in the V of the open shirt, the firm swell of her breasts. He drank in her beauty with eyes that were heavy-lidded. She looked straight ahead and did not turn to him until they were at the rustic bench at the back of the bunk-house.

Then she said: 'Let's sit down, Perce, and you can say your little piece.'

She sat down, smoothing her skirt almost primly with her hands.

He did not sit down but placed his one foot up on the bench and leaned over her.

'I think you can guess what I mean tuh say, Miriam,' he said softly. 'I said it once before and got nowhere. Now I'm sayin' it again, and this time I want a straight answer.' He smiled, and his face lost its handsome blankness and became like that of a merry boy. 'I think I'll get my answer all right,' he said.

The girl's dark eyes widened a fraction. 'Go on,' she said.

There was a slight pause. He reached forward and took hold of her hand.

'I want you to marry me, Miriam,' he said.

Her mouth opened. She pulled her hand away. She seemed to struggle for words. Then she said: 'Perce – don't you know? Nobody's supposed to know but everybody seems to—'

'Know what?' His voice was sharp.

'I'm going to marry Kit Hamden. Our engagement will be announced at the barbecue tomorrow night.'

He stood erect, looking down at her. Wide-eyed she looked up at him. She did not like the strange look in his blue eyes.

But his voice was surprisingly quiet when he said: 'No, I didn't know. You led me to believe—'

'I didn't lead you to believe anything,' she interrupted sharply. 'We've always been friends – I told you the first time that I wouldn't marry you. I didn't change my mind—'

'You acted as if you had—'

'I didn't. I never acted more than a friend to you.'

'You played with me,' he said softly. 'Pretended – an' all the time you meant to have Hamden. He was your father's choice, wasn't he, he'd wormed his way in—'

142

'He was my choice!' said the girl hotly.

The man went on monotonously: 'All the time you knew – an' you pretended. Playin' with me. Stringin' me along.'

His voice was a mere whisper now: 'After all that. After all I've done—'

'What have you done?' she said.

He lunged forward suddenly and grabbed her arm. He was grinning mirthlessly. 'You'll know maybe,' he said. His voice rose, his blue eyes glowed. 'I could kill you,' he said. He pulled her up towards him.

'Perce,' she said. 'You're mad! Let me go!'

For answer he crushed her roughly to him. His one hand sought her throat. He pressed, jerking her chin up. He tried to kiss her mouth. With sudden strength she twisted her body from his grasp and pulled herself away from him.

'You vile beast,' she gasped, and struck him across the face with her clenched fist.

He recoiled. Then he stood still, his face blank again, his eyes hooded. A little trickle of blood ran from the corner of his mouth. Without a word he turned on his heel and strode away.

When Miriam got round to the front of the bunk-house he was riding down the trail. Her brow was clouded. She decided not to tell her father or Kit of the incident.

She went into the cookhouse beside the ranch house. John Wang, the Chinese cook, was preparing a meal for those men who would come in to supper. He greeted her cheerily. He obviously had not seen anything. She got the supplies she had come for. These were for her father's tea which she always prepared herself. She returned to the ranch house.

Later, as she laid the table, she watched the trail. Twilight was falling. She saw some of the men ride in, Kit amongst them. They went to the bunk-house. Although Kit was always welcome to meals in the ranch house he always insisted on having them with the men as he had from the start, despite the fact that many of the men disliked him. They considered him too domineering. Miriam was well aware of this. Her lips curled scornfully. Kit had more guts and initiative than any of them. His only fault was his hair-trigger temper. But she had a temper, too. They would be well matched.

The yard was empty again. Her gaze travelled across it, past the corral and out to the trail once more. Two more men were coming along it. She watched them as they came nearer in the twilight. Then suddenly she stiffened. She went right up to the window, peering through to make sure she was not mistaken. Then she turned and went in the back room to her father.

As Bancroft and Otson dismounted by the steps old Burt came out on to the veranda. In his hands he held a shotgun.

'You won't need that, Mr Burgoyne,' said Bancroft. 'If we came with warlike intentions we wouldn't ride up like this.'

The old man saw the sense of that. He lowered the gun slightly but still looked wary.

Bancroft said: 'We've got a mighty long story to tell yuh. Can we come in?'

'I don't know what you want,' said the old rancher. 'But I guess you'd better come in an' state your business. I hope you won't abuse my hospitality. Just remember my men are within call.'

'We will,' said Bancroft. 'An' you'd seem heaps more hospitable if you put away that gun.'

The old man glared at him. But he lowered the gun entirely and stepped aside to let them pass.

'Straight ahead, gentlemen,' he said with a sudden return to courtesy.

The two men had been sitting with her father for about twenty minutes when Miriam went in with a tray of drinks. They were so engrossed in conversation that they did not seem to notice her.

Old Burt was saying: 'I'll send some of my own men in with you in case the townsfolk cut up rough. Many of them still think you are wanted men, you know. If I were you I should pin those badges where they can be seen.'

'You can send your men in, just in case of interference,' said Bancroft. 'But please remember I want to take him alone.'

The old man nodded. 'I understand.'

The two visitors seemed to notice Miriam for the first time, and they greeted her.

'Miriam,' said her father. 'Would you mind sending Wang for Kit Hamden?'

The girl nodded and left the room.

Ten minutes later Bancroft, Otson and Hamden rode at the head of a band of men taking the trail to Elkanville. Not so far behind them rumbled the buggy bearing Burt Burgoyne and his daughter. The old man did not mean to miss anything. As usual, his daughter had insisted in being in on it too. He knew better than to refuse her. Anyway, she always handled the horses better than he did.

Of the three men who rode up front, deputy marshal Otson was the first to speak.

'I hear you're gettin' spliced, Kit,' he said.

Hamden said: 'Yeh. My, it sure gets around.'

'The ol' man told us,' said Bancroft.

'I wuz surprised to find you got up to him without bein' pumped full o' lead,' said Hamden. 'An' now I find he's been tellin' you the family news.'

'Congratulations,' said Otson.

'Thank you.'

Silence again as they jogged along. The muffled beating of the horses' hoofs on the hard trail seemed part of the silence. None of the little band had much to say. They were grim and thoughtful.

It was Hamden who softly voiced their thoughts.

'I've thought there was something fishy about Maddison for a long while. He's too mealy-mouthed for my likin'. The way he butters up to the ol' man sticks in my craw – but I never thought he was bad as that. I never dreamt – why did he do it?'

Bancroft answered him softly: 'He wanted money and the power that goes with it – an' Miss Miriam.'

Hamden was not offended. 'He would never have had Miriam. He never stood a chance.' He was stating a fact.

Night was fully upon them as they cantered into the main street of Elkanville. A brilliant moon turned the street into a river of silver, across which horses and riders threw shadows like black phantoms. Windows were lit up. Light streamed at intervals from the doors of the Buckeye Bar as thirsty cowboys passed in and out. They took the horsemen to be a bunch riding in from the range for an evening's spree. Until an old-timer paused under the horses' noses and recognized Bancroft and Otson. He gave the alarm. In a surprisingly short time the little band were surrounded by people and were compelled to halt right outside the Buckeye Bar.

THIRTEEN

Sheriff Perce Maddison sat in his chair behind his desk. His head was sunk on his chest. He still wore his hat, but it was pulled down over his eyes.

He seemed to be asleep, but he was only brooding. The whole tortuous edifice of deceit, hate and greed he had built up around himself these last few months was now crumbling in dust around his ears. All his plans, all his ambitions against which nothing had been allowed to stand in his way, everything was collapsing.

All the wealth was as nothing now the person with whom he had planned to share it was lost to him. Even now, he realized what he could do with it – what power it could buy for him. But not the power he so greatly desired – to be master of all this territory with Miriam by his side.

Yes, he could still have the power that money could buy, and all the comforts, too, in some other place.

But he could not go from here and leave Miriam to another man. Doubtless both of them were laughing at the way he had been joshed along. He'd stop their laughter. And give the whole town something to laugh at before he left them.

He lifted his head. He looked at the gun-belt and his twin Colts slung on the desk beside him. He shrugged. He had plenty of time! None of the fools in this town were very good at figuring things out. Maybe he'd find them another scapegoat – another Gimpy Bancroft. Then would be the time to get to work on Kit Hamden – and his lady-love. A sudden spasm of pain creased the brown, handsome features. The eyes blazed hotly. Then just as swiftly the face became expressionless again.

He was thinking deeply now, his face blank, the eyes hooded. Only slowly did the sounds from outside begin to swim into his consciousness. There was something going on down by the Buckeye Bar!

He rose to his feet, reaching for his gun-belt.

The office door opened suddenly. A voice said: 'You won't need those, Perce.'

'Gimpy!'

Bancroft's draw was a thing of wonder. The sheriff's hand stopped in mid-air over the gunbelt as he felt himself menaced by a blue-barrelled Colt. The eyes above it were cold and merciless, the eyes of a man-killer.

'Just push 'em from the desk, Perce,' said the lean man. 'I want to talk to you.'

The sheriff complied. The gun-belt, with its twin guns, clattered to the floor.

'The jig's up, Perce,' said Bancroft. 'I've come to take you in.' He flipped back his vest with one hand, revealing the little silver badge pinned to its underside.

Maddison did not say anything, but sank into the chair behind his desk.

Bancroft holstered his gun, hooked another chair with his foot, and sat down straddle-legged facing Maddison.

The sheriff said. 'You're crazy. What've you got against me?' But it was a very half-hearted bluff. The speaker seemed apathetic.

Bancroft said: 'Jest a slight case of five murders, that's all. An' I've got plenty of proof.'

Maddison took a packet of cigarettes from his pocket. Bancroft recognized the brand – the same as he had found in the nest of the sniper who shot Otson. Yeh, everything was tying up now. This man before him, this man who had been his boyhood friend, was a cold-blooded murderer. In all his years of man-hunting the marshal had never come across a worse one, or one so deceptively calculating. Right now, he seemed cool, tired-looking.

He tossed the packet of cigarettes across the desk. Bancroft took one. They lit up. Both dragged deeply and blew out the smoke until it was a blue haze between them. The sheriff spoke first – slowly, dispassionately, conversationally.

So, for the last time, like friends again, they talked. The once so taciturn Maddison seemed relieved to be able to unburden himself. However, Bancroft thought he detected a faint tone of gloating in the level voice.

Maddison told of how he had met old Uncle Jeb with his gold and, acting almost on an impulse, had killed him. Of how, while still carrying the gold, he met Shorty Matthews. Afterwards, Shorty blackmailed him until Maddison, catching him in an unguarded moment while he was drunk, picked a fight with him and blasted him into silence.

Shorty's pard, Mike Calhoun, got very cocky and insulting, and Maddison feared maybe he knew or suspected something. He awaited a favourable opportunity and shut his mouth, too. His own lackadaisical manner was a pose; he made his decisions in a split-second and acted on them swiftly and thoroughly. He seemed very proud of this fact. He told his tale in a flat, monotonous, utterly unemotional voice. Bancroft realized he was dealing with a man whose mind was sick. But a man who, though now deceptively docile, was still very dangerous.

Outside the office now, very little sound could be heard. Both men sensed the atmosphere of waiting as they lit cigarettes again and the sheriff talked on.

He was very sorry he had had to make Gimpy the scape-goat. You might say Gimpy had almost brought it on himself.

Very cunningly, Maddison sold the gold at intervals in different parts of Mexico, and salted the money away in various American banks. Bancroft told him of the slip he made with old Guido. Maddison shrugged. It was all water under the bridge now; he was finished.

Through all his narrative he did not once mention Miriam Burgoyne. Finally, he confessed to the killing of Big Lou and Long Jack. They had been found shot on the trail just outside the town a few days back. They knew the sheriff had left the way clear for the mob to get Bancroft. They asked him for a loan, and he figured maybe they were beginning to suspect. He couldn't do much else but kill them.

Maddison slapped one hand hard down on the top of the desk. 'There it is, Gimpy,' he said, and he was smiling.

His other hand appeared, holding a small derringer. Bancroft had been expecting something; but even so, he was almost caught. He threw himself desperately to one side as the little weapon cracked spitefully. The slug

151

plucked his shirt at the shoulder.

The chair went over with a clatter. Bancroft sprawled against the desk. He rose to his knees and pushed. The desk went over. The derringer spat again, but the slug went harmlessly into the air as Maddison staggered. The oil-lamp fell to the floor with a crash of breaking glass. The light flared for a moment, then went out. The room was plunged into pitch-blackness.

Bancroft rose on one knee, his gun in his hand. There was a scuffle, then a Colt boomed, the flashes picking out the moving form of the sheriff, who had evidently retrieved his gun-belt.

Bancroft threw himself flat as the slugs fanned the air around him. Then he was retaliating, spraying the room with lead, seeking his moving target. Flying lead pinged and ricochetted from the iron-barred grill of the door that led into the jail-house. Bancroft figured his enemy was somewhere over there. He was cursing himself for being careless. He might've known Perce would have something up his sleeve – which was probably the very place in which he had kept the derringer.

The booming of shots echoed and died. The place was full of acrid gun-smoke. And there was silence. Bancroft tensed himself, his gun ready. He strained his ears.

There was a faint murmur from outside. The shots had been heard. But inside the dark, shuttered room the silence was like that of a tomb.

Bancroft wondered whether he had hit his opponent. He began to slither slowly forward. Another almost imperceptible noise followed his own movement and, even as he pressed the trigger, he was throwing himself forward.

Bancroft's head hit the desk as Maddison fired rapidly

again. The lean man was dazed by the sudden blow. He was only vaguely aware that the door which led into the jail-house opened then banged shut again.

He acted instinctively, mechanically. Rising to his hands and knees, he almost threw himself across the intervening space. He reached upwards, caught hold of the handle of the door, swung the door open. Then he dived through flat on his belly, his one gun forward and blasting; the other was empty in his hand.

Shots answered his, the bullets smacking into the door behind him. A blast of cold air was wafted down the passage, then another door banged.

Bancroft sat up. He was all right now. He reloaded swiftly, then rose to his feet and ran down the passage. He opened the outer door, letting in the night air once more. He was greeted by the sound of thudding hoofs.

The black silhouette of retreating horse and rider was plain in the moonlight. Bancroft fired twice. The horse stumbled and went down. The rider disappeared from sight.

Half-crouching, Bancroft ran forward. Flame stabbed from behind the bulk of the fallen horse. Bancroft felt a searing pain in the bicep of his left arm. It went limp; his left-hand gun dangled in lax fingers. He went down on one knee, firing with the other gun.

Maddison rose to his feet, and weaving, stooping, began to run.

Bancroft flung another shot after him and thought he saw him stagger. He put down his gun and tore a piece of cloth from the sleeve of his shirt. He rolled the sleeve back. Maddison's slug had creased him. He wrapped the strip of shirting round it, tightening it with his teeth until

153

it cut into the flesh. He flexed his fingers, then grabbing both guns, rose and ran after the fugitive. He was the cool, perfectly trained man-hunter now.

He spotted Maddison again. The fleeing sheriff had reached the end of the houses. This was the quiet part of town. The ground began to rise now to the ghostly slopes and crude headboards of Boot Hill – a place humped by pitiful mounds of earth; a place of decay and stunted trees, where cats prowled, and occasionally coyotes.

Maddison turned and fired. Bancroft felt the wind of the slug. He raised his gun to retaliate, but the sheriff was already out of sight around the corner of the end house.

There were shouts from the street, denoting that the crowd had spotted the fleeing man. Bancroft turned the corner of the house himself. The crowd was advancing sluggishly. Bancroft held up his hand. They slowed down. He heard the voices of Otson and Kit Hamden. Then the crowd stopped altogether. This was Bancroft's show.

Bancroft turned away from them, turned towards his quarry. As he did so Maddison's gun barked again. Instinctively, the lean man ducked. The slug smacked into a log wall behind him. Still Bancroft held his fire and ploughed on.

Boot Hill was bathed garishly in moonlight, the stunted misshapen trees, the crazy headboards above the mounds, the few flowers and the waving grass – all black and etched in silver. For a moment, Maddison, huge and black against the skyline, seemed to tower above it all. Then, even as Bancroft raised his gun, the silhouette became foreshortened – then vanished.

Crouching, Bancroft was among the graves himself – as

154

the sheriff, from the cover he had found himself, opened up.

The lean man cursed between his teeth, his lips quirking as they tightened. He fell flat on his stomach. So Perce was going to stay and fight it out was he?

He raised his right-hand gun, swinging it around in a wide arc, fanning the hammer with his left-hand until the chambers were empty, and his injured arm throbbed with pain. The bullets screamed in the stillness, the gunsmoke blew into his eyes and nostrils, the night was made hideous with sound that echoed and re-echoed along the slopes and out into the breezeblown range. Then the night was silent again as Bancroft reloaded.

There was no sound from the dark patch of boulders that screened Maddison. He was well-covered, but, even so, he might have been hit. Then again, he might be playing possum. Both guns now loaded, his wounded arm throbbing, his eyes smarting and his mouth dry, Bancroft lay and waited.

A few seconds passed, but to a man not used to waiting they seemed like hours. Finally, he lifted his left-hand gun. He rose to his feet, firing rapidly as he did so. Then fell flat again. From the rocks came answering shots. A figure rose. A slug plucked at the hair on Bancroft's bare head.

He rolled, catlike, and rose again, shooting deliberately. Maddison's hat flew from his head. His blond hair gleamed in the moonlight as he rose to his full height and, like an actor in the limelight, began to descend the slope towards Bancroft.

The lean man's blood sang with savage satisfaction as he went to meet him. For a moment he felt a strange regard for his erstwhile friend, a lead-slinging fool who, to

155

the last, was a worthy opponent.

Simultaneously, like a pre-arranged signal that was instinctive between them, both men opened up.

The blond-headed giant seemed to pause, to wilt a little. Then he came on with a sudden convulsive jerk.

A slug clipped Bancroft's gammy leg. It gave way beneath him and he went down on one knee. Maddison was nearer now, his face plain in the moonlight, the eyes glaring, the teeth bared. A mere target for the guns of the merciless lawman who opposed him.

But Maddison's aim was plain. He meant to get that lawman before he dropped himself.

Although Bancroft's body burned with pain his brain was ice-cold. Even as Maddison raised his gun again, the lawman fired coolly and deliberately. *Three shots.*

Maddison's body shook as if from three terrific blows. His face was horribly contorted now. He tried to raise his gun once more, then let it drop. His body went with it, crumpling. He went on his knees beside a grave, almost as if praying, then, with a convulsive movement, fell forward on his face. He lay still. The night was suddenly quiet.

Bancroft rose to his feet and, dragging his leg painfully, went over to the body.

He turned it over. The face was more composed now, handsome again. Tendrils of blond hair clung wetly to the forehead.

'*Adios*, Perce,' said Bancroft.

He turned and began to wend his way slowly, haltingly, between the graves and headboards, down the hill to the waiting crowd.

The moon shone just as brightly the following night,

although the body of Perce Maddison, late sheriff of Elkanville, lay cold and stiff in Three-ton Thurston's undertaking parlour. The town was almost deserted. Everybody was out at the barbecue that was being thrown at the Curly W.

It was common knowledge now that the shindig was to celebrate the engagement of Miriam Burgoyne to Kit Hamden. Although old Burt wasn't altogether an all-fired popular man he certainly knew how to throw a party. Everybody was invited and, despite individual opinions of the Burgoyne regime, everybody went.

There were free eats, free drinks and a rootin'-tootin' danceband that had come all the way from Austin. The big yard in front of the ranch house had been swept and garnished and surrounded by tables and benches. There was a wide clear space in the centre and lanterns suspended on poles to illuminate everything. And up on an improvised stage sat the band, swinging it out.

All the honoured guests sat on the veranda with the 'old man' himself. And right now it did not seem at all incongruous to see up there along with Pete Otson, Doc Penders, Three-ton Thurston and others, the lean form of the once-hated trouble-shooter, Gimpy Bancroft. The aforesaid Gimpy had his arm in a sling. His long, homely face was serene but a mite thoughtful-looking as he watched the dancers, dragged at his cigarette and occasionally had a pull at the glass at his elbow.

It was getting pretty late when he turned to his pardner, Pete Otson, and said something, and Pete passed it on to old Burt. The old man seemed to be arguing a little, he even leaned forward and chewed the fat with Bancroft – but, eventually, he rose. The two men rose with him and

157

followed him into the house.

Half an hour later the old man came out on to the veranda again, alone. Nobody, except maybe a couple of drunks who were shunning the limelight for a while, saw the two pardners get their horses from the corral and mount up. They walked the beasts to just outside the aura of light which proclaimed the festivities and there, unseen, watched for a moment.

The band was playing a jig. Little by little the couples dropped out and, as if by common consent, drifted from the floor, until only one last pair of dancers were left, Miriam and Kit, the betrothed couple. They paused on finding themselves alone.

The crowd whistled and cheered, egging them on, stamping their feet and clapping their hands in time with the music. Needless to say, the dance continued.

They were a handsome pair, straight, supple, virile examples of young womanhood and manhood, their eyes shining, their teeth flashing. Who could help but wish them well?

In the darkness Pete Otson said softly: 'Wal – there they go, bless 'em.'

Bancroft was silent for a moment, his face still wearing the thoughtful look. Then he grinned and said: 'Yeh.'

He turned his horse's head. 'You ridin' along, Pete?'

'Yeh, I'm ridin' along, Gimpy.'

They turned in line. Side by side they rode out on to the trail.